I0799350

ANCIENT AMERICA'S LOST GIANTS

DISCOVERING ANCIENT AMERICA

ANCIENT AMERICA'S LOST GIANTS

XAVIANT HAZE

Rosen YA

This edition published in 2018 by
The Rosen Publishing Group, Inc.
29 East 21st Street
New York, NY 10010

Additional end matter © 2018 by The Rosen Publishing Group, Inc.

All rights reserved. No part of this book may be reproduced in any form without permission in writing from the publisher, except by a reviewer.

Library of Congress Cataloging-in-Publication Data

Names: Haze, Xaviant, author.
Title: Ancient America's lost giants / Xaviant Haze.
Description: New York : Rosen Publishing, 2018. | Series: Discovering ancient America | Audience: Grades 7–12. | Includes bibliographical references and index.
Identifiers: LCCN 2017002100 | ISBN 9781499466768 (library-bound)
Subjects: LCSH: America—Antiquities—Juvenile literature. | Giants—America—History—Juvenile literature. | Mounds—America—Juvenile literature. | Copper mines and mining—America—History—Juvenile literature. | Excavations (Archaeology—America—Juvenile literature. | Human remains (Archaeology—America—Juvenile literature. | Paleoanthropology—America—Juvenile literature.
Classification: LCC E21.5 .H39 2018 | DDC 970.01—dc23
LC record available at https://lccn.loc.gov/2017002100

Manufactured in the United States of America

First published as Ancient Giants of the Americas by New Page Books/Career Press, copyright © 2017 Xaviant Haze

CONTENTS

INTRODUCTION

In a time when human beings are able to access unlimited amounts of information in the blink of an eye, it would seem that all ancient myths and mysteries should be on the verge of being solved as either fact or fiction. Yet despite the technologic utopia most people live in, the simple truths of bygone eras appear to be harder than ever to prove. Is this because the evidence simply doesn't exist? Or is there a worldwide archeological cover-up going on that is determined to keep the status quo going? Despite the fact that the theory of evolution is just that—*a theory*—and one that's constantly challenged and bombarded by new discoveries, it's a theory that for better or worse has become the standard "end all, be all" of accepted academia. But what happens when new evidence threatens to upend this universally accepted theory? Most of the time it's ridiculed, swept under the rug, or flat out ignored. Take for instance the theory that ancient giants once roamed the earth thousands or even hundreds of years ago. It's a duly noted footnote of mankind's history, verified and spoken about by all ancient cultures from various parts of the globe. Yet despite being mentioned in the Bible and other ancient holy texts, the idea that a forgotten race of ancient giants existed in times immemorial has been relegated to the realms of fantasy and nothing else. This seems a bit harsh considering that new species of humans have been popping up with mass infrequency throughout the past decade. Take for instance the enigmatic Red Cave Deer People, a mysterious new species of ancient humans identified from cranial bones, jaw bones, and teeth fragments discovered in 2012 in two Southwest China cave sites.[1]

In 2015, fishermen off the coast of Taiwan discovered a 4-inch fossilized human jawbone belonging to a new kind of primitive human that once inhabited Southeast Asia 190,000 years ago. Scientists named the discovery "Penghu man," as the bone was recovered in a fishing net near the remote Penghu Islands. The Penghu man bone is the right side fragment of a lower jaw with four complete teeth still attached. Scientists have concluded that the jawbone isn't related to the two other forms of *Homo erectus*, the Peking man, or Java man, and that it belongs to an unknown separate race of primitive people altogether.[2] The Penghu man jawbone is also unrelated to the "Hobbit" race Homo floresiensis, whose fossilized remains were discovered on the nearby Indonesian islands in 2003. The Hobbit race, like those depicted in J.R.R. Tolkien's *Lord of the Rings* fantasy adventures, were alive and well in Indonesia as recently as 18,000 years ago, despite having a brain the size of a grapefruit. Thanks to their teeth, scientists have been able to confirm that Hobbits once roamed the earth as a completely separate species.[3] However, new theories concerning the Hobbits are putting this status in jeopardy, as they are now being related to a much more diminishing role of the human ancestor, perhaps as a smaller

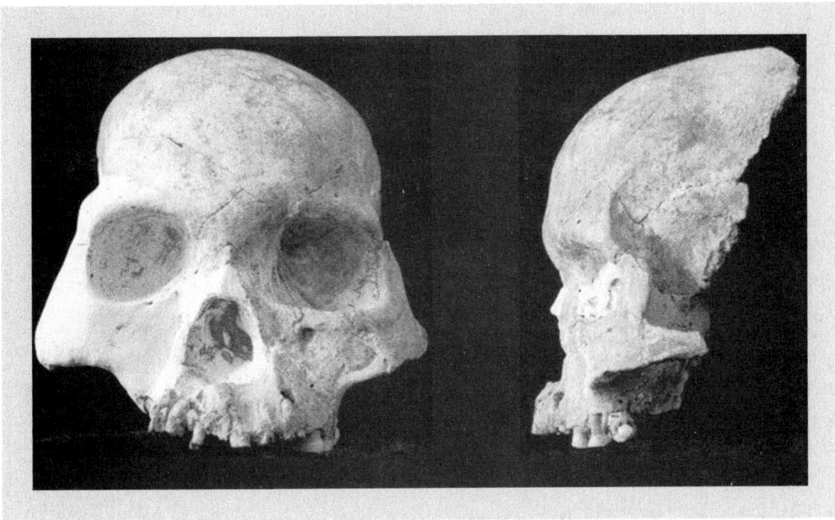

Red Cave Deer People skull anterior and lateral.

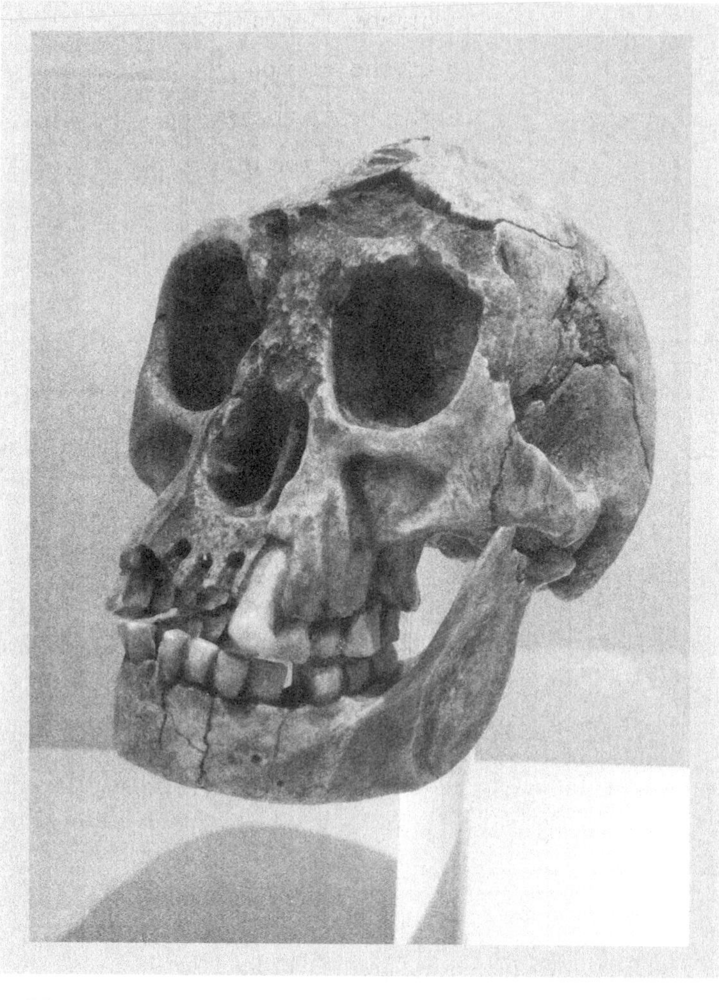

Homo floresiensis *skull displayed at the Natural History Museum of Senckenberg, Switzerland.*

medically challenged abnormality rather than a completely separate species. But the speculation, mystery, and controversy remain, as it seems the Hobbits were around as recently as 12,000 years ago before their sudden disappearance. Curiously enough, this is the exact same time period in which the pre-flood worlds came to an end and the cataclysmic events of the Ice Age began. This means that the Hobbit was around the same time as the other pre-flood hominin species, marking their existence as both exciting and incredibly confusing. We know that modern humans made it to Australia around 50,000 years ago; to get there, they passed through Africa, which puts them in the general area of Southeast Asia and the Indonesian Flores Island where the Hobbit existed. This means they must have lived alongside any sentient species that crossed their paths during this time. And since humans have a way of destroying everything around them, who is to say that we didn't wipe the Hobbit off the face of the Earth too? And whoever was left of that tiny race was then destroyed by the natural disasters that upended Earth during the Ice Age. It's no secret that this destructive timeline happens to match the extinctions of other human species, like the Neanderthals and the mysterious Denisovans, who disappeared shortly before the last Ice Age and after modern man entered the picture.

But more new species of ancient humans are being discovered. Take for instance the H. Naledi, a mysterious dwarf species similar to the Hobbit discovered deep in a South African cave in 2015. The bones of this species have been dated to at least a half a million years old, adding another mystifying branch to the family tree.[4] What about the *Homo rudolfensis*? Ever heard of them? It's another strange human species discovered in Kenya in the 1970s whose remains are

The cave on Flores Island where specimens were discovered.

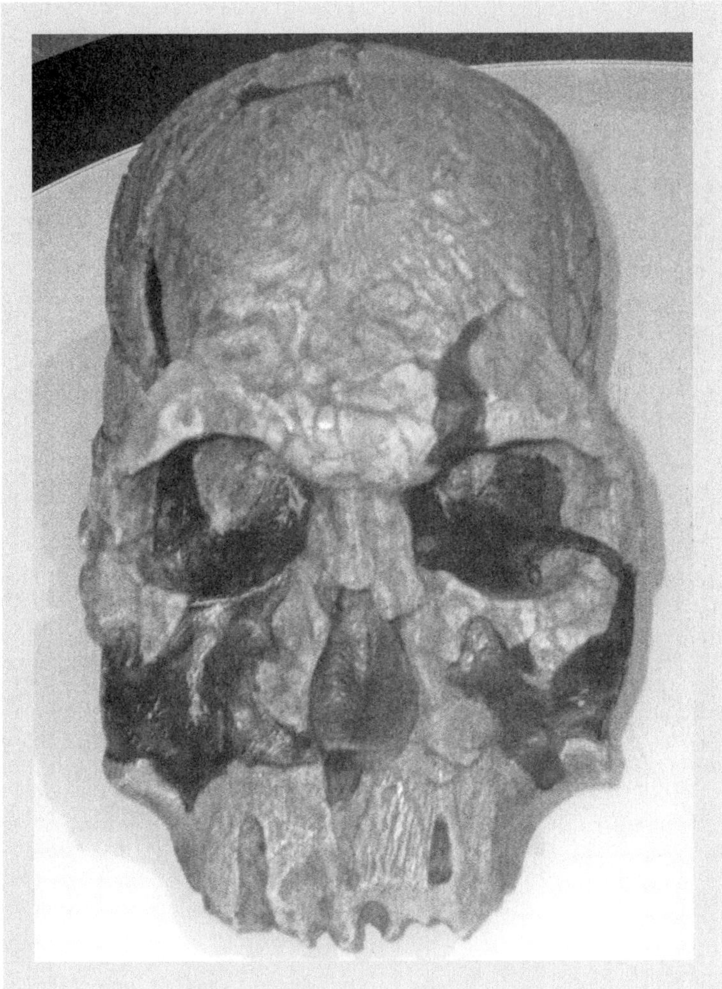

Homo rudolfensis *skull reconstruction displayed at the Museum of Man in San Diego.*

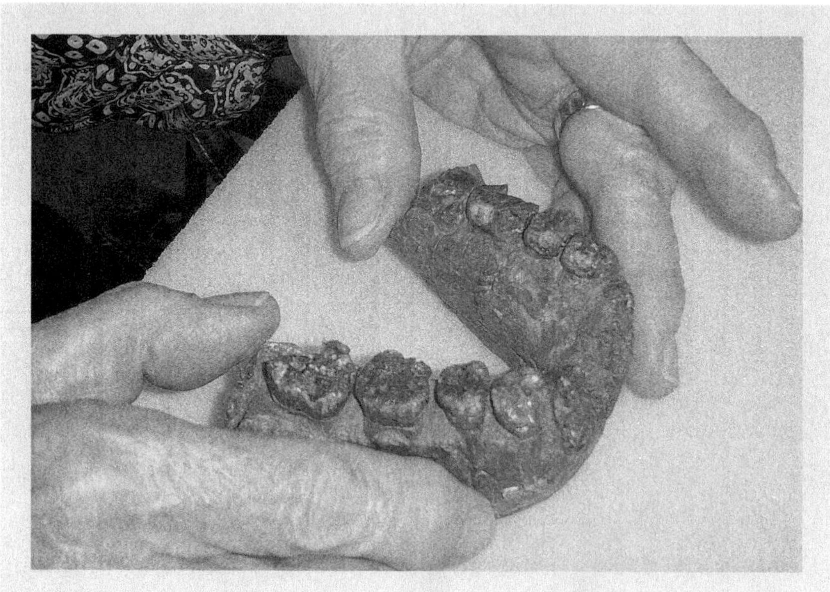

The oldest fossil of the genus Homo.

more than 1.9 million years old.[5] That's about 2 million years shy of yet another newly unearthed species of humans discovered in the Afar region of Ethiopia in 2015. A team of archaeologists made the discovery of hominin jaw bones and teeth belonging to an unknown race of humans dating back 3.5 million years ago. This find means that this species wandered around at the same time as several other early human species from the Australopithecus family. "Lucy" is the most famous direct ancestor; her bones were discovered 42 years ago and it is estimated that she lived 3 to 3.8 million years ago.[6] This new addition has been named *Australopithecus deyiremeda,* which translates to "close relative" in the language spoken by the Afar people that live in the area of its discovery.

Then there's the mysterious Denisovans, a cousin of the Neanderthals that once roamed the Earth alongside *Homo sapiens* more than 60,000 years ago. It turns out that the genomes of the Denisovans contain a segment of DNA that comes from another species completely unknown to science. DNA tests also discovered that the Denisovans mated with a mystery species from Asia that is neither human nor Neanderthal and also had huge giant-like teeth.[7] Adding more mystique to this conundrum was the discovery of four hunting spears that date back 400,000 years. These expertly crafted spears were found in a coal mine outside of Hanover, Germany, and are considered to be the oldest and most complete hunting weapons ever discovered. However, orthodox academia and conventional scientists stick to the Darwinian model, which argues that humans didn't begin hunting until 40,000 years ago, despite the contradictory evidence.

Advancements made in recent DNA tests have been shattering all kinds of established ideas concerning the theory of evolution. It's

Australopithecus family.

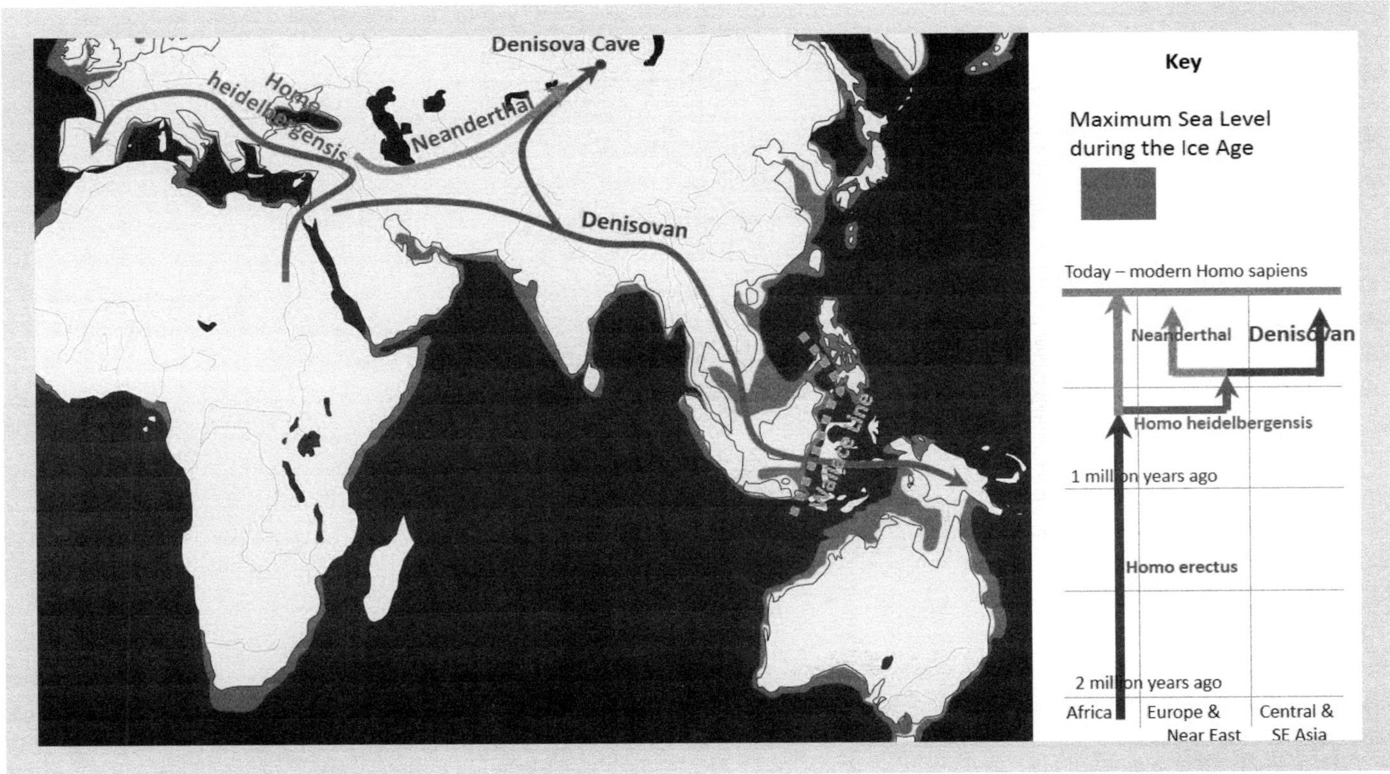

The spread and evolution of the Denisovans.

been revealed that we carry more than 145 "alien" genes that have no direct links to our ancestors, squashing the notion that evolution relies solely on genes passed down through the ages.[8] Mathematical codes in our DNA cannot be explained by evolution and some researchers have even suggested that they are the result of a genetic engineering experiment conducted by an alien race millions of years ago. Proof of these alien experiments might be contained in the mysterious elongated skulls discovered in the Paracas region of Peru. DNA tests on these skulls confirmed that they had mitochondrial DNA with mutations unknown in any human, primate, or other animals.[9] Curiously enough some of these elongated skulls have been discovered with heads full of red hair! So here's *another* new human-like species that is similar yet vastly different from either Homo sapiens, Neanderthals, or Denisovans. All of these mysterious species once roamed Earth thousands and even millions years before the rise of smart phones, selfie sticks, Netflix, and striped toothpaste. But where are the ancient giant bones? Sadly this is the one species that refuses to resurface. Could there possibly be evidence hidden away in the basements of the Smithsonian and at the homes of private collectors, historians, occultists, and antiquarians?

The legends of ancient giants continue to entertain from beyond their hidden graves while interest in them has never been greater. There was even a six-episode show on the History Channel dedicated to searching for them. Pouring over written accounts from the early 19th century, a clear pattern emerges that portrays early America as home to more than just American Indians. Discoveries of giants and giant mounds of a forgotten era were constantly being discovered and openly talked about years before the suppressing dogma of

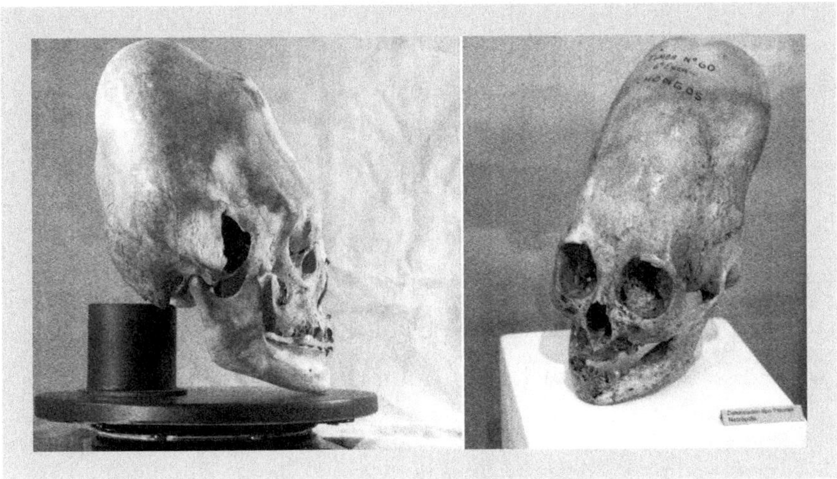

The elongated skulls of Paracas, Peru.

Darwinism came crashing about. But not all of these giants were in the dirt, as a few chiefs from certain tribes remained visible. As the Western world was opened up by the exploring conquistadors, some shocking discoveries were made, including firsthand accounts that revealed many giants were still roaming around in the Caribbean and remote areas of Mexico, South America, and the southern United States. In fact, ancient giant bones were presented to travelers who were astonished to find proof that validated biblical tales and legends on the other side of the known world. Obviously not all of the giants were destroyed in the great flood. . . .

CHAPTER 1

Mysteries of the Lost Copper Mining Giants

As the conquistadors marched forward to alter the course of history, they left behind written records describing their encounters with the surviving race of ancient giants. This race had mixed with the Native Americans and shrunk significantly throughout the ages, as most of the reported accounts put their height anywhere between 7 to 9 feet. This is a lot smaller than the rumored 12- to 20-foot giants of antiquity who supposedly built the world's great megalithic structures like Stonehenge. Currently the tallest man in the world is Turkey's Sultan Kösen, who measures an astonishing 8 feet, 3 inches. The tallest man ever in recorded history was the American Robert Wadlow, who was measured a staggering 8 foot, 11 inches. That's an inch shy of being a true-to-life 9-foot-tall giant. However, mainstream science blames Wadlow and Kösen's super tall statures as a rare case of gigantism brought on by a pituitary gland issue and not because of wayward giant genes. But the proof of giants can be found in more places; they are most prevalent in museum archives,

Robert Wadlow's shoe, size 25, compared to a normal men's size 12.

indigenous mythological histories, and also in stone monuments and lost out of place artifacts that have been improperly dated or suppressed by academia.

Ancient astronaut theorists claim that a race of giants was created after the alien gods saw the how beautiful the Earth's women were and decided to impregnate them. This meddling of the gene pool created an ancient race that became the dominant life form on the planet. These gods soon grew intolerant of the giants who had become nefarious and wicked and decided to destroy them with earthquakes and floods. This story has since been rehashed and retold in various forms by basically every ancient civilization in recorded history.

As for the giants of the ancient Americas, one might be able to trace their mysterious origins all the way back to the Bronze Age copper traders that once inhabited the icy regions of the upper Midwest. The Bronze Age was a period in history epitomized by the usage of bronze from the times of 3200–600 BCE. It's an important milestone in human history with one major issue: Where exactly did all the copper come from? Obviously we know that Europe had its own Bronze Age, but archaeologists have reluctantly begun to accept that a lot more copper was used than the amounts attributed to European mines. The answer, of course, is America. Science has determined that large quantities of copper were mined in the Midwest during the European Bronze Age. However, nobody knows what happened to the copper after it was mined there. To mainstream archaeology the answer is unquestionably "no," as they remain adamant that there was no transoceanic contacts in the Bronze Age. Perhaps they should look at the recent scientific literature, which provides ample amounts of evidence that the best copper of the era couldn't have possibly come from Europe.

More than 10 tons of copper oxide ingots recovered from a Bronze Age shipwreck off the coast of Turkey were found to be extraordinarily pure at more than 99.5 percent. Only Michigan Copper, which was mined in enormous amounts during the Bronze Age, is of this purity. Other similar ingots have been discovered in Crete, Sardinia, Cyprus, Turkey, Bulgaria, Israel, Egypt, and England. Copper is one of the most common metals on the face of the Earth, however, copper that registers over 90 percent is extremely rare and has only been discovered in the mines of the American Midwest. Historians estimate that half a billion pounds of copper was mined by ancient miners throughout a period of a thousand years in ancient Michigan alone, yet nobody knows where that Michigan copper went. However, if you visit London's British Museum Bronze Age axe exhibit, you'll be informed that from about 2500 BCE, the use of copper, which was formerly limited to areas of Southern Europe, somehow swept through the rest of the continent, despite the fact that nobody knows where the copper in Europe came from.

American Indian legends claim the copper was mined by a seafaring red-haired race of giants. Legends of northern Wisconsin's Menomonie Indians say the ancient mines were first identified by magical stones possessed by the giants. When these giants pointed their enchanted stones at the ground a ringing sound would echo off the stones, detailing the location of the copper ore deposits like some sort of ancient metal detector. Besides their mining operation this mysterious giant race of miners left no other evidence of their existence behind; not one burial or crematory deposit exists at or near any of the ancient Midwestern mining sites. Maybe these giants only worked during the summer seasons, returning home across the Atlantic or moving south during the more frigid winter months. This would explain the absence of any buildings or copper melting facilities that would be required for longer stays. But where did this copper mining knowledge originate from? There isn't an established answer.

North America has no clear-cut source for this copper mining culture that, according to the natives, were a race of sailing vagabond giants. When questioned about the mines the natives only knew of their existence in distant memories and legends. Yet amazingly a few pieces of historical evidence associated with these mysterious miners have been found. In 1660 a French missionary named Claude-Jean Allouez stumbled upon a 12-inch copper statue that depicted a man with a beard, which is pretty peculiar considering that American Indians couldn't grow beards.[1] Another giant-linking artifact is the remarkable rock carved petroglyph (circa 1640) detailing one of their sailing ships, which can be seen at Copper Harbor, Keweenaw Peninsula, Michigan.[2] During this thousand-year period of copper mining it would make sense that some of the miners branched out to explore the western areas of the American continent. They might have even begun to interbreed with the native populations during this time.

A fascinating discovery related to the red-haired giants comes from the Lovelock Cave on Lake Lahontan in Nevada. In 1924 a pair of bat guano farmers discovered a group of mummified giants buried with fishnets, duck decoys, and shell art in a cave in Lovelock, Nevada. The various sea-associated relics found in the burial point back to a time when Nevada was flush with abundant rivers, lakes, and water sources. A giant handprint and extremely large 15-inch sandal was also discovered in the cave, and one of the giant skulls was prominently displayed in the small town's museum up until 2010 before disappearing into memory due to a change in museum policy. The giant handprint, discovered in 2013, was recently vandalized in an attempt to erase its existence. The local Paiutes, a tribe indigenous to parts of Nevada, have an oral tradition about a race of unfriendly and cannibalistic red-headed giants that came to the Lovelock cave area from unknown lands thousands of years ago.[3]

It seems these mysterious giants trekked and sailed across the American West at least 3,000 years before the Lewis and Clark Expedition. They even brought back a shrub typically found in the rainforest gulches of the Pacific Northwest. This strange shrub with giant leaves and spiny stems doesn't appear anywhere else east of the Rocky Mountains. This plant has been used medicinally for hundreds of years to treat diabetes, tumors, and tuberculosis, and it appears that it was brought to the Lake Superior region in ancient times and planted at the exact same spots where the giant miners were excavating copper. These giants were well traveled; one of their arrowheads was discovered near a megalithic stone circle in the seaside town of Cornwall, England. When the farmer that discovered the arrowhead sent it to the British Museum for identification, the museum shockingly replied that the arrowhead was more than 5,000 years old and came from Michigan.[4]

The fact that the arrowhead was found near a megalithic monument is even more intriguing considering that megaliths and giants

Entrance to Lovelock Cave near Lovelock, Nevada.

have become synonymous throughout history. America has a megalithic history as well, albeit one rarely discussed. In the northeast, ancient dolmens and stone works that align to the solstices can be found in New Hampshire, New York, Vermont, Massachusetts, and all the way up into Canada and Nova Scotia. When the English Pilgrims began to settle the Northeast they were shocked to find the same types of megalithic structures they had known in Bronze Age Europe. The governor of Connecticut in 1657, John Winthrop Jr., a prominent member of the Royal Academy in London, wrote lengthy papers about these ancient stone forts and dolmens of New England. He compared them to the stone wonders found on the misty hills of Avebury in Southwest England. When asking the local Algonquian Indians for information regarding these Northeastern megaliths, Winthrop Jr. was disappointed that they didn't know any more than he did and attributed their mysterious origins to an ancient race of long-lost giants.[5]

Eventually, the 20th-century dawned and the reports from Winthrop Jr. and others documenting pre-Colombian voyages across the Atlantic were subsequently left out of the history books. This meant that the possibilities of megalithic works found in America, which mirrored those of ancient Europe, were relegated to the list of "impossible," despite the obvious proof of their existence. Academia would soon just ignore the topic altogether, even when Harvard-educated genius Barry Fell wrote books about the subject in the 1970s in an effort to shift the paradigm. The establishment went out of their way to destroy him in the hopes that his information would never reach the enlightened minds of the future. They did a good job, as Fell's theories aren't taught in schools and

America's Stonehenge in Salem, New Hampshire.

his books have been assigned a permanent home in the dusty basements of most libraries.

In the Ohio Valley, an area rampant with mounds and giant bones, there is a Bronze Age henge similar to those discovered on the British Isles. Used as solar markers and calendars, a henge is usually a circular or oval-shaped area that's confined by earthworks comprised of timber, stone circles, monoliths, burials, and earthen mounds. These megalithic stone circle henges frighten archaeologists because it destroys their false timeline of history. From the *Bureau of Ethnology, 12th Annual Report West Virginia*:

> Below the mouth of the Kanawha the caving in of the bank of the Ohio had exposed a wall of stone, on some of the slabs of which were rude totemic and other marks made be some pecking tool. Careful excavations revealed a circular enclosure about 100 feet diameter, inside measurements. The wall was composed of angular slabs of various sizes from the hills nearby and averaged 25 feet across the base by 3 1/2 in height. Many of the stones bore evidences of fire, the spaces between them (they were laid flat with joints broken) being filled with charcoal, ashes, and earth, separate or mixed . . . The sediment from the overflows has accumulated to the depth of about 5 feet since the wall was built, and its existence was never suspected until exposed as above stated by the falling in of the bank. This may not be aboriginal work . . . The doorway lintel in the lower mound is distinctively European.[6]

There is also a solar henge complex in Newark, Ohio, which consists of a stone circle that tracked the moon and the movement of the sun. Recent excavations around the ditch of the henge unearthed a pile of burnt wood; carbon dating tests revealed a date between 1000 and 800 BCE, placing the henge in a timeframe that doesn't jive with the historical paradigm put forth by established academia. In fact, the entire state of Ohio is home to a diverse amount of strange American anomalies, from mounds to giants to mysterious ancient tablets. It seems that the upper Ohio Valley was once host to a lost forgotten race of giants. Could this be where the giant miners of Michigan decided to call home when they weren't hammering out copper? Excavated mounds in Chillicothe, Ohio, produced art ranging from metal copper birds to numerous intricately carved effigy pipes and copper masks. One report even listed the burial of an ancient giant decked out in copper armor:

> The party under the direction of chief Putnam, of the ethnological department of the exposition, who had been making excavations of the mounds in Ohio for several months met with rare success near Chillicothe in making one of the richest finds of the century in the way of pre-historic remains. While at work on a mound near Chillicothe, five hundred feet long, two hundred feet wide, and twenty-eight feet high, they found the massive skeleton of a man encased in copper armor, the head covered with an oval-shaped copper cap, the arms dressed in copper, with copper plates on the breast and

An Indian mound at Chillicothe, Ohio.

> stomach, while on each side of the head, on protruding sticks, were wooden antlers ornamented with copper.[7]

Mound excavations done in the late 1800s revealed even more astonishing finds related to giants, including huge rust-corroded iron helmets, 39-pound copper axes, and elaborate conch and pyrula shell–inspired necklaces imported all the way from the Atlantic Ocean. Mounds in Bainbridge Ohio, revealed mummified bodies draped in pearl-covered robes, half a million fresh-water pearls, and more giants decked out in copper helmets and armor. Hundreds of newspaper reports commented on the vast amounts of giant discoveries that were being made in Ohio during the settling of America, similar to this account from the *Stevens Point Daily Journal* in 1886:

Ohio Account of Nine-Foot Giants

> It is very evident that at an early day in the history of this country, this section of Ohio was an important camping ground for the American Indian. And, indeed, discoveries are frequently made, which lead people interested in the matter of prehistoric America to believe that a race of mankind, superior in size, strength, and intelligence to the common red man of the forest, flourished not only along the coasts East and South, but right here in southern Ohio. There are in this county several burying grounds, and two of them are located five miles west of this city, near Jasper, one on the farm of Mr. William Bush and one on Mr. Matthew Mark's farm.

> In a conversation with a gentleman who has seen [skeletons] unearthed at the Mark bank, we were told that many dozens of human skeletons have been exhumed since the bank was first opened. Some of these skeletons have been measured, and the largest have been found to be nine feet long and over. At one time ten skeletons were exhumed. They had been buried in a circle, standing in an erect position, and were in a comparatively well-preserved condition. One remarkable fact about all the skeletons unearthed at these places is the perfect state of preservation in which their teeth are found to be. Not a decayed tooth has been discovered, and this would seem to indicate that these people naturally had excellent teeth or some extraordinary manner of preserving them.[8]

On September 26th, 1889, the *Cincinnati Courier Gazette* reported:

Gigantic Man Buried Alongside a Colossal Panther

> About five feet above this layer, or nine feet from the summit of the mound, was a skeleton of a very large individual who had buried by the side of it the bones of a panther. . . . The skull of this panther was very large, teeth very long and sharp. It would take a mound builder of a great deal of nerve to attack a beast of this size if he had nothing but a stone hatchet and bow and

> arrows to defend himself with. Just below this skeleton and lying on the layer of buried bones was a medium-sized personage who had buried around his neck in the manner of a necklace, between his upper and lower jaw, 147 bone and shell beads. The shell beads were made from the thick part of Conch and Pyrula shells. These shells must have been carried from the Atlantic Ocean, as they are ocean shells, and not found inland, or the tribe to which the man belonged may have traded with tribes near the ocean and thereby got the beads.[9]

While digging in preparation for the World's Fair in Ohio, workers were shocked to discover the copper clad burial of an ancient giant monarch. The November 21st, 1891 edition of the *Ohio Enterprise* read:

> Warren K. Morehead and Dr. Cresson, who have been prosecuting excavations here for the past two months in the interest of the World's Fair, have just made one of the richest finds of the century in the way of pre-historic remains. Those gentlemen have confined their excavation to the Hopewell Farm, seven miles from here, upon which are located some twenty-odd Indian mounds. On Saturday, they were at work on a mound 500 feet long, 200 feet wide and 28 feet high. At the depth of 14 feet, near the center of the mound, they exhumed the massive skeleton of a man encased in copper armor. The head was covered in an oval-shaped

> copper cap, the jaws had copper mouldings, the arms were dressed in copper, while copper plates covered the chest and stomach and on each side of the head, on protruding sticks were wooden antlers ornamented with copper. The mouth was stuffed with genuine pearls of immense size, but much decayed. Around the neck was a necklace of bear's teeth set with pearls. At the side of the male skeleton was also found a female skeleton, the two being supposed to be man and wife. Mr. Morehead and Mr. Cresson believe they have at last found the "King of the Mound Builders."[10]

However impressive this once-mighty lost race of copper-mining giants had been, by the time the Spanish conquistadors came to the Americas they were nothing more than a fleeting memory and shadows of bad fairy tales at the end of Native American folk stories.

CHAPTER 2

Giants of the Southeast

When the Spanish conquistadors came to the new world, they were expecting to find gold—not deadly encounters with giants. Unfortunately, most of what the Spanish thought was gold turned out to be Tumbaga, a mixed bronze alloy painted to look like the precious metal the conquistadors were so desperately seeking. In fact, the conquistadors wound up finding more hardships than actual gold as they plundered, murdered, and enslaved their way through the Western Hemisphere all in the name of God. Looking to spread Christianity to the savages they encountered was their way of reconciling the fact that they were destroying thousand-year-old cultures. But the conquistadors were the marching armies of Spain, and the heads of Spain were interested in only one thing: gold. So imagine the shock and disbelief of the conquistadors upon their first encounters with giants; it must have been a truly mind-blowing site to behold since the average height of the Spanish was around 5 foot, 4 inches at the time. (Keep in mind that these giants were around 6 to 9 feet in height, making battles against them a very daunting task.)

The Spanish encounters with giants were scarce, as most of the natives were of normal size, but chiefs of certain tribes were indeed giants. They made these claims to keep a certain giant bloodline alive, as an archaic set of mystery genes was passed down among tribe members ages ago. Some of these giant Indian chiefs were now the inheritors of that lost race of red-headed giants who once mined copper on the Bronze Age shores of Lake Superior. With their forefathers already long buried the great chiefs of the 1500s knew it wouldn't be long before their race would suffer the same fate, as the arrival of the conquistadors signaled a certain doom.

Conquistador and explorer Pánfilo de Narváez had already conquered Jamaica and Cuba but failed to capture Native settlements in the sticky jungles of Northern Florida; he retreated back to port at Tampa Bay with less than half his men. Starving and with no gold in sight, his men moaned with empty bellies as they marched back to shore. Those who survived were lucky enough to not perish in the Florida jungles or get picked off by arrows flung from native archers. When a starving Narváez finally made it to the harbor he discovered that his ships had all but vanished. With no other option, he and the remaining soldiers made makeshift rafts and attempted to sail back to Cuba, but ran headfirst into a menacing storm and were never seen again. The last man to see Narváez alive and tell of it was Alvar Nuñez Cabeza de Vaca, who was one of only four men to miraculously survive the grueling expedition. After a harrowing nine-year journey that nearly killed him multiple times Cabeza de Vaca published his amazing story in 1542 and it quickly became a sizzling Spanish best-seller. Cabeza de Vaca's story had all the exciting elements found in page-turning classics, plus extra special ingredients such as battles in strange Florida jungles with giants:

> When we attempted to cross the large lake, we came under heavy attack from many giant Indians concealed behind trees. Some of our men were wounded in this conflict for which the good armor they wore did not avail. The Indians we had so far seen are all archers. They go naked, are large of body, and appear at a distance like giants. They are of admirable proportions, very spare and of great activity and strength. The bows they use are as thick as the arm, of eleven or twelve palms in length, which they discharge at two hundred paces with so great precision that they miss nothing.[1]

Ten years later, Hernando de Soto followed in Narváez's footsteps by sailing nine ships into Tampa Bay with the intent of conquering Florida once and for all. As they ventured inland, they encountered various tribes, each with a giant that reigned as chief. The conquistadors kidnapped these chiefs and infuriated local tribes, which banded together to fight under the tomahawk of the giant Chief Copafi of the Apalachee. The uprising sparked a war that lasted for weeks. de Soto eventually chased Copafi deep into what would be modern-day Tallahassee before finally capturing and executing the giant rebel. Hernando de Soto's encounters with giants continued as he pushed further inland with more than 600 men and 200 horses. Rodrigo Ranjel, de Soto's private secretary, wrote about the mighty

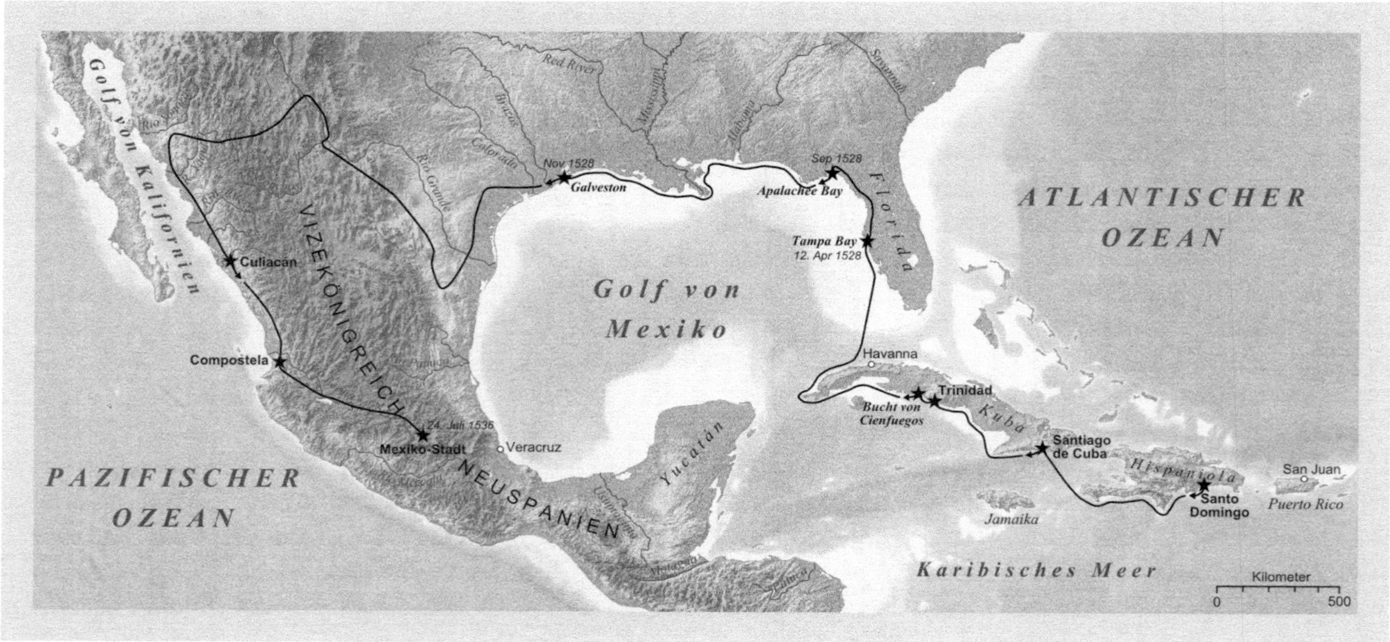

The expedition of Cabeza de Vaca.

giant chief Tuscaloosa and the chief's giant offspring who greeted the weary conquistadors as they marched into muggy Alabama. Ranjel wrote:

> We reached a hamlet, which though rightfully under his scepter, oft with treacherous arms His lawful sway had stubbornly withstood. A giant monarch, Tuscaloosa, ruled the neighboring kingdom, and he sowed abroad among these subjects of his brother-prince Disloyalty and discontent. Here came to meet us from the pathway to the West, a warrior, naked as a god from heaven scorning the fleecy drapery of the clouds; only upon his brow were scarlet plumes Plucked from the ibis, while his careless hand swayed a spear lightly. Seeing him, we paused, Dumb with amazement. For, though but a youth Still in his April dawns, he towered on high, a great-limbed giant: heads of tallest men reached only to his breast . . . taking up our march, after three days we reached the little town where the chief tarried. Pitching first our tents, the monarch next we sought, and soon descried ensconced before his wigwam on a mound, an hundred of his peers surrounding him. A giant mightier than his son.[2]

De Soto and 15 soldiers entered Tuscaloosa's village, and were treated to a few days' worth of colorful war dances before convincing Tuscaloosa to peacefully join them on their quest toward Mobile. It was even hard finding a horse for the giant chief to ride upon as he was so large that his feet ended up dragging on the ground. While on the trail, two of de Soto's soldiers turned up missing and the returning scouts returned to warn de Soto about the many Natives that had gathered for rebellion. De Soto rode through a welcoming committee of painted warriors, dancing women, and flute-playing children and entered the town with his fellow soldiers, Tuscaloosa, and the chief's entourage. The outnumbered conquistadors were now surrounded by more than 2,000 Native American warriors who were hiding behind the town's walls. Sensing the danger they were now in, de Soto demanded that his men be unharmed as Tuscaloosa laughed in his face before disappearing into a hive of Indian warriors. The arrows began raining down on de Soto and his men as they retreated from the village while Tuscaloosa escaped. After regrouping and revising their strategy, de Soto and his men gained entry into the village, killed Tuscaloosa's giant son, set fire to the place, and massacred the city's inhabitants. Tuscaloosa was soon captured by the conquistadors and hanged to death in full view of the town's smoldering inferno. The city of Tuscaloosa in Alabama is named after the giant chief. As de Soto and his men marched deeper west they were finding fewer giant chiefs and more massive mysterious mounds. Some of these mounds contained the remnants of the lost race of giants that once ruled the Americas.

Anglo-American settlers who came to Florida in the mid-1800s were well versed in local urban legends claiming that an ancient race of giants once inhabited the sun-soaked state. Some of these early settlers even claimed to have seen thousands of giant skulls floating on the surface of Lake Okeechobee. When the drought hit in 2007, Lake Okeechobee's water level receded so low that it revealed a cemetery full of skeletons that were at least 7 feet in length. Some of their massive skulls even showed signs of intentional deformation like the famous elongated skulls of Paracus, Peru, mentioned earlier in the book. It's a strange coincidence that the giant chiefs of the Calusa Indians of South Florida were known as the *Paracus-te*, which means "the people of Paracus." This is an area in Peru home to a vast desert and harsh arid conditions; it's also home to numerous graves of elongated skulls and the infamous Nazca lines, which can only be seen from the sky. South Florida is a long hike from the highlands of Peru; maybe they flew there? The following is a 1925 news article from Florida that may shed some light:

Huge Skeleton Found in Florida

> Discovery of a skull, one forth larger than that of the normal modern, together with bones indicating a probable height of not less than seven feet, leads to speculation over theories of a giant race believed to have once inhabited Florida. The portions of the skeletons were found by workmen grading a road near Charlotte and Lee county lines. The bones are believed to be those of a male. The specimens are to be shipped to the Smithsonian Institution.[3]

Given the measurement it's safe to say the skelton was about 7 and a half to 8 feet tall. More 8-foot-tall giants were discovered by fisherman in Miami as reported in the June 9th, 1936 issue of the *New York Times*:

> Tale of human skeletons eight feet long embedded in the sand of an uninhabited little island off of the southern tip of the Florida mainland was brought here today by three fishermen. They exhibited a piece of one skull containing six teeth. E. M. Miller, zoologist at the University of Miami, said the mandible was that of a man and was probably seven hundred years old. "It is entirely probable that this find might be important," he commented, "but I could not tell anything about it unless I had the measurements or additional information." The men said the skulls were unusually thick, the jaw protruded and the eye sockets were high in the head.[4]

The first state geologist of Florida, E.H. Sellards, believed that the area's original inhabitants were a race of giants that dwelled in the southeast more than 125,000 years ago. He oversaw an excavation in Vero Beach that unearthed giant skeletons more than 12 feet in height. As reported in 1917:

> That human beings inhabited the North American continent more than has been conclusively proven through a recent discovery in this state by E. H. Sellards, state geologist, and Prof. Oliver P. Hay who have made a study of the fossil. Though their opinions are not fully concurred in by other scientists, they are positive that

> their researches have been thorough and there is no room for a mistake. The discovery was made several months ago, and though nothing of a definite nature had been given out until recently, it is now officially stated that human bones intermingled with those of the mastodon, saber tooth tiger, and many other extinct animals that formerly ranged this hemisphere have been found. The deposit was found near Vero. That the human beings were of enormous size is evidenced by the bones. It is thought that some were ten or twelve feet in height. Some excellent specimens of the skeleton of these gigantic men have been found, some of them locked in the deadly embrace of great animals, with strange weapons of bone clutched in skeleton hands a foot long.[5]

Sellards and Hay were soon in the academic crosshairs as their discoveries threatened the evolutionary modeled timeline. Unsurprisingly they were forced out of their positions and relocated far away from Florida. Their discovery of giant human remains in the Pleistocene period in North America flies in the face of established history, which claims that giants never existed in the first place, let alone non primate–like humans living alongside extinct ancient animals. Proof of this was discovered in the Vero Beach excavation site more than 90 years later by an amateur fossil hunter who discovered a carved mastodon bone. After three years of studying the fossil, science has claimed it to be "the oldest, most spectacular and rare work of art in the Americas."[6] However, there was no mention of the ancient giant skeletons discovered in the same

Earth strata, which were conveniently lost shortly after arriving at the Smithsonian in 1945.

This wasn't the first time carved mastodon bones have caused a sensation. In the 1960s amateur archaeologist Juan Camacho discovered an engraved mastodon bone near the Valsequillo Reservoir in the Mexico City area. A team from Harvard showed up and began excavating the site, eventually finding some of the oldest spearheads in the world and more carved bones. The team put forth peer-reviewed studies postulating the age of the artifacts at more than 40,000 years, which was three times older than the official 12,000-year-old date for the first Americans—an exciting discovery for everyone involved. But when the United States Geology Survey (USGS) geologists examined the artifacts and the site they had a much more mind-blowing age, dating the site and the artifacts at more than 250,000 years old![7] This would radically alter everything we've ever been taught since, according to mainstream academia, humans weren't around that long ago in general, never mind killing mastodons and carving art on their bones. The establishment deemed that the dating was impossible despite the science proving otherwise and promptly dismissed and ignored the matter altogether. The discovery site in question soon became off limits and has been ever since, preventing any further excavations or investigations into this fascinating part of our ancient history.

So if they suppressed *that* part of history, why stop there? More giant skeletons were discovered on a tiny island off the shores of Tampa Bay in a zone once traversed by ravishing conquistadors. The following extract is from the *Lawrence Journal-World* on August 5th, 1927:

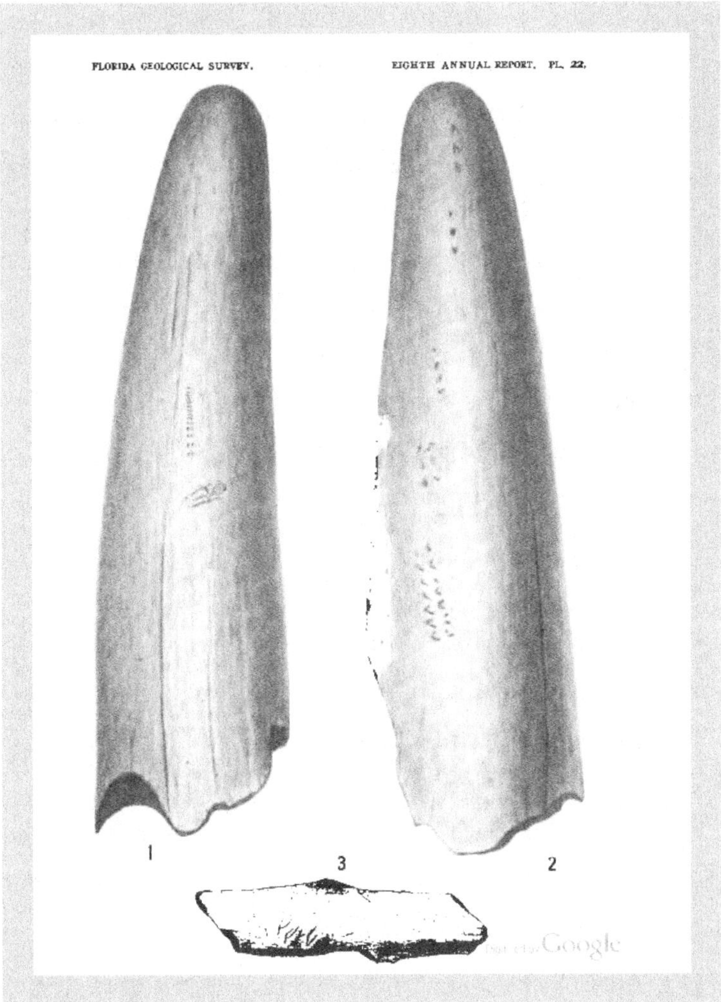

Illustration of mammoth or mastodon tusks with marks presumably made by humans. Found by E.H. Sellard at Vero man site in 1916.

> Giant Indians who roamed Florida swamps 500 years or more, living on shell foods which they cracked with their teeth, is a picture unfolded by archaeologists who have delved into a burial ground on a Gulf Island near here. The skeletons were discovered on a small section of land, where a lone fisherman has lived for years. Scientists estimated that the bones are at least 500 years old and are remains of a tribe known as Caribs, natives of the West Indies. They are believed to have inhabited the state and adjacent islands before the Spaniards in Florida. The skulls, larger than those of current history, battered and crushed, indicated tribal battles. The jaw and teeth are unusually large. Likewise are the body, bones, indicating the Indians of past ages were veritable giants in comparison with those today. Mounds similar to the one in which the bones were unearthed are common in this state. The bones have been sent to the Smithsonian Institution for further examination.[8]

Once again, the bones were sent to the Smithsonian and never seen again. In 1911, Florida canal builders discovered an unknown race of 7-foot giants when they attempted to destroy a mound that was in their way. It was a cool winter's eve when workers in Boynton Beach demolished the 15-foot-high mound that was covered in greenish plant shrubs and mahogany vines. The following extract details some of that process.

> Boynton, Florida, Dec. 6. There was much surprise and excitement when the workman began removing the soil of the mound, to find it was an ancient burial place of some unknown people, the history of which has not been learned. About one half of the mound has been removed in the grading of the roadway and in that were skeletons of about 50 people, all placed with care and precision with heads toward the apex of the mound. The bodies were placed in layers with an amount of sand between and ocean sand had been carried in to cover them. Amber beads, broken crockery, and scissors, rusted apart, were among the articles found buried there. One skeleton which was found intact, measured seven feet from crown to toe. The bodies had been buried such a length of time that many of the bones crumbled when exposed to the air and moved about.[9]

The Tocobaga Indians that inhabited the Tampa region were also referred to as "giants" by the European settlers of Florida.[10] In 1932, another 8-foot giant was discovered off Cape Sable near Homestead and was given to the University of Miami, which promptly lost the remains. An undisturbed 2,500-year-old graveyard of giant bones was discovered by divers at the bottom of Silver Springs near Ocala, Florida, while mounds in St. Petersburg unearthed an ancient race of giants more than 9 feet tall.[11] It's safe to say that if the conquistadors attempted to excavate these mounds their minds would have been blown to smithereens.

The neighboring state of Georgia also has its fair share of anomalous giant history as well. But it's the nation of Georgia, once part of Soviet Russia, that is sending shockwaves to the establishment with recent bone discoveries that threaten to overturn the theory of evolution once and for all. Archaeologists have unearthed six ancient skeletons dating back 1.8 million years, and these incredibly well-preserved Georgian bones are the earliest humans ever found outside Africa.[12] Coincidently bones of a giant man were discovered in a cave in the nearby Georgian city of Borjomi, and Russian news reports about the discovery estimated the man to be around 9 to 10 feet tall, while the skull was more than three times the size of an average human skull.[13] Unsurprisingly these giant bones have gone missing.

Recent DNA and archaeological tests have also proven that a great cataclysm known as the "Younger Dryas" event was caused by a comet strike that happened at the end of the last Ice Age more than 12,000 years ago.[14] Scientists studying the DNA of ancient Europeans found evidence of an unexplained population shift when local hunter-gatherers were nearly replaced by an unknown group from another area. Researchers from the Max Planck Institute for the Science of Human History in Germany made the intriguing discovery. After studying the 40,000-year-old mitochondrial genomes of 35 European hunter-gatherers, the Institute's Johannes Krause reported, "We uncovered a completely unknown chapter of human history. A major population turnover at the end of the last Ice Age." Adam Powell, another Max Planck Institute scientist adds, "Our model suggests that during this period of climatic upheaval, the descendants of the hunter-gatherers who survived through the last glacial maximum [Ice Age] were largely replaced by a population from another source."[15] Could this source be the mysterious red-headed giants that once flourished during the Bronze Age? Five of their giant Bronze Age axes, twice the size of those normally discovered, were found in a field in Jutland, Denmark, in 2015. This discovery by Danish farmers adds to the total number of Bronze Age axes discovered in Northern Europe to 10, although the previous five were only about half the size of the giant Danish axes.[16]

Back in 16th-century America, the conquistador Pedro de Salazar was near the coast of Georgia looking to enslave American Indians when he discovered a tribe of peaceful giants. These American Indians resided on one of the various islands that litter the coastline between Georgia and Cape Fear, North Carolina. Salazar and his men wined and dined with the Natives in a place named "Island of Giants" by Spanish historians.[17] After a few days of rest and reconnaissance Salazar decided it was time to pack up and take the giants back with them. They resisted but were forced on the voyage back to Hispaniola. More than half of the giants died on the quest back to the islands and the remaining giants died shortly after being forced into slavery in Puerto Plata. These giants of Georgia were taller than the local Arawak-Lucayans, who were already considered huge to the tiny conquistadors. It was later discovered that these giant Georgian Indians had established trade routes and made many voyages to the Caribbean, specifically the Bahamas. When other conquistadors returned to find Salazar's Island of Giants they didn't find any more tribes and abandoned coastal searches of Georgia for inland treks.

An important giant discovery was made in Cartersville, Georgia, in 1886 when a team from the Smithsonian was excavating the Tumlin mounds. Inside one of the mounds they found a vault inscribed with strange undecipherable hieroglyphs, which housed the skeletal remains of a 7-foot-tall giant:

> Several years ago an Indian mound was opened near Cartersville, Ga., by a committee of scientists from Smithsonian. After removing the dirt for some distance a layer of large flag-stones was found, which had evidently been dressed by hand, showing that the men who quarried the rock understood the business. These stones were removed, and in a vault beneath them was found the skeleton of a giant, measuring seven feet and two inches. His hair was coarse and jet black, and hung to the waist, the brow being ornamented with a copper crown. The skeleton was remarkably well preserved and was taken from the vault intact. Nearby were found the bodies of several children of various sizes. The remains of the latter were covered with beads made of bone of some kind. Upon removing these the bodies were found to be enclosed in a network of straw or reeds, and underneath these was a covering of the skin of some animal. In fact, the bodies had been prepared somewhat after the manner of mummies and will doubtless throw new light upon the history of the people who reared these mounds. On the stones which covered the vault were carved inscriptions, and if deciphered will probably lift

> the veil which has enshrouded the history of the race of giants which undoubtedly at one time inhabited the continent.[18]

All the evidence from this important discovery was shipped back to the Smithsonian and promptly lost. These Tumlin mounds are known today as the Etowah mounds and associated with the local Etowah Indians who, before their extinction, claimed that they had nothing to do with the building of the mounds. It's pretty clear that we can associate the mounds with that race of giants that once inhabited America. Mound excavations in the 1880s at the Etowah complex produced a stunning giant more than 14 feet tall, which unfortunately has also gone missing. This insane discovery was reported by the *New York Times* in 1886:

Monster Skull and Bones

> Cartersville, Ga., April 4. The water has receded from the Tumlin Mound Field, and has left uncovered acres of skulls and bones. Some of these are gigantic. If the whole frame is in proportion to two thigh bones that were found, their owner must have stood fourteen feet high. Many curious ornaments of shell, brass, and stone have been found. Some of the bodies were buried in small vaults built of stones. The whole makes of mine of archaeological wealth. A representative of the Smithsonian institution is here investigating the curious relics.[19]

Mound B at the Etowah Indian Mounds archeological site in Georgia.

The mounds of Georgia unearthed more giant skeletons along with other various artifacts and shell arts unassociated with local Georgian tribes like the Cherokees. In fact, when questioned about the mounds, the Cherokees possessed no information whatsoever about the race that built them.

One of the most ancient archaeological sites in North America is the mound complex built on the Mississippi River bayou at Poverty Point, Louisiana. The complex, which has been dated back to 1500 BCE hosts six enormous mounds that were aligned to predict the vernal and autumnal equinoxes. Although a visit to these mounds today will not mention anything in relation to giants, 19th-century news articles tell a different story. More than 700 mounds once dotted the landscape of Louisiana, and most of them unearthed ancient giant bones like those reportedly discovered in Winnsboro, Louisiana in 1882.

> Skeletons of a race of giants who averaged twelve feet in height were found today by workmen engaged upon a drainage project at Crowville, near here. There were several score, at least, of the skeletons and they lie in various positions. It is believed they were killed in a prehistoric fight, and that the bodies lay where they fell until covered with alluvial deposits due to the flooding of the Mississippi River. No weapons of any sort were found, and it is believed the Titans must have struggled with wooden clubs. The skulls are a perfect state of preservation, and one

> of the [j]aw bones [is] large enough to fit around a child's body.[20]

The southeastern state of Tennessee was also host to mysterious mounds and ancient giants. In 1874, a mound south of Elvis's Memphis stomping grounds found a giant skeleton buried with colorfully painted terracotta vases. Although some "giant" discoveries in Tennessee turned out to be mastodon bones of other ancient animals (such as sloths), a good portion of the discoveries were those of an unknown lost race of giants that had been mostly forgotten. Besides, mastodons never buried themselves with human artifacts such as masks, pots, and wampum bead arts. Tennessee's old stone fort in Manchester is another mysterious ancient monument once again falsely attributed to the local natives. The old stone fort looks more like an old stone wall that might have been constructed by traveling Welshman or Phoenicians, or it might even be old enough to be associated with giants. The March 30th, 1872, issue of the *Hartford Weekly Time* details this finding:

Race of Giants Found In Underground Tomb Under "Old Stone Fort" in Tennessee

> Near this city is a cave commonly known as "Bone Cave," from which have been brought, at various times, by boys and other persons who have tried to explore its hidden recesses, human bones of unusual size. The popular legends of the people are to the effect that it is somewhat connected with the people or race which

> created the "Old Stone Fort," which stands a short distance to the west of the town. A few days since some boys discovered an almost entire skeleton of mammoth size. The bones of the forearm were nearly twenty inches long, while the bone of the lower part of the leg was longer than an ordinary man's limb, foot and all. The jawbone of this giant would slip over the face of an ordinary man. . . . This passage [of the cave] looks as if it had been cut from the solid rock by the hand of man and gives rise to the hypothesis that at some time, far back in the dark ages, this cave was used by a race of men—giants if you like—that built this stone fort and the mounds and that this underground passage led from the fort to the cave, a mile distant.[21]

Giant skeletons were also found in a mound at the nearby town of Ripley, Tennessee, as reported by the *Logansport Reporter* on July 3, 1903:

> **Indian Mound Near Tennessee Town Yields Remains of Gigantic Men**
>
> Ripley, Tenn., April 23. (AP)—Skeletons of three gigantic men buried by a forgotten race have been unearthed by a fisherman digging in an old Indian mound near here. Tribal finery in which they were interred was recovered intact. One of the skeletons bore ivory beads and a long ivory ornament. The other was

> decorated with copper beads and designs of bone and mica. Two were found near the surface. Further down the largest of the skeletons was discovered in a sitting position on a carpet of ashes. Pottery, one piece containing the bones of an infant, was found nearby. It was in a fine state of preservation. Indian mounds abound in this section but hitherto none had yielded skeletons the size of those found by the fisherman. He has offered them to the Tennessee Historical Society at Nashville.[22]

About an hour and a half away near the town of Franklin, more giant bones were unearthed by a resident farm owner searching for water springs on his property. From the *Tennessee Western Weekly*, November 11, 1845:

> There have been recently dug up in Williamson county, Tennessee, seven miles from Franklin, the bones of a giant and no mistake. We have conversed with an intelligent and enterprising gentleman of our city, who has seen, examined, and purchased an interest in the skeleton. From him we derive the following facts: A Mr. Shumate was boring for water near his residence, upon a hill of considerable extent and eminence, situated in a rocky, mountainous section country, where the bones were discovered about 60 feet beneath the surface. They were immediately exhumed, and were found embedded in a strata of the hardest kind of clay which had apparently filled an extensive cavern or opening in the rock . . . No doubt rests in the minds of any who have seen

> or examined them, that these bones belong to the genus homo. All the larger and characteristic bones are entire, and the skull, arms and thigh bones, knee pans, shoulder sockets and collar bones remove all skepticism as to their humanity. The whole skeleton, we are informed, is about 18 feet high, and must have stood full 19 feet "in his stockings" (if he wore any).[23]

These bones were later assembled to create a traveling exhibit, which was first showcased in a downtown Nashville movie theater and then moved to a museum in New Orleans for public display. Newspapers across the country were hailing the discovery as proof of an ancient giant race, possibly from Atlantis. The excitement soon turned to ridicule, however, when a scientist from the Louisiana Medical College debunked the Williamson County giant as nothing more than mastodon bones. Despite this debunking, additional giant bones and Indian giants were waiting to be discovered in the southwest as more conquistadors like Coronado made the trek in search of everlasting glory and fabled lost cities of gold.

CHAPTER 3

Coronado and the Giants of the West

IT WAS A JOURNEY full of conquest, wonder, adventure, danger, and heartbreak. It was a journey inspired by tales of lost cities of gold—cities once ruled by a race of giants in times immemorial and tales that inspired more than 300 conquistadors, 1,100 American Indian allies, and more than a thousand animals to embark on an epic journey across hot arid deserts and rugged mountains. The tales inspired the man who led them: a 30-year-old Spanish playboy by the name of Francisco Vázquez de Coronado. A man from a noble family, Coronado was born in Salamanca, Spain, in 1510 and attended the famous university there before ditching his studies to join his conquistador buddies in Mexico. While in Mexico, Coronado married a wealthy woman who was able to secure him a high-ranking position in the Spanish army. In 1538, Coronado was named governor of New Galicia (a Spanish province in Mexico) and he soon began hatching a plan to get rich and famous.

First, Coronado financed a mini-expedition to El Dorado by sending the knowledgeable monk Marcos di Niza on a northern journey of exploration. Marcos had been with Pizarro during his conquest of the Incas in Peru where he learned about the fabled golden-walled seven cities of Cibola, more commonly known as El Dorado. After finding gold in Peru but failing to locate El Dorado, di Niza learned that the legendary source of Incan gold was in a land much farther north of South America. Figuring that it was somewhere in Mexico, the monk followed the trail to the Spanish-ruled Mexican province of New Galicia where he acquired the final bits of information regarding the location of the city. After dazzling Coronado with his tale, di Niza was sent out to find the city with some Indian guides and the black freeman Estevanico (one of the survivors of the ill-fated Narvaez expedition). Estevanico had travelled and lived with American Indians of the north for many years, spoke a variety of languages, and claimed to know exactly where the legendary lost city was located. With Coronado's blessing di Niza and his team of treasure hunters began their quest for El Dorado, heading north into modern-day Arizona, a landscape both strange and picturesque with fertile valleys, abundant streams, and snow-capped mountains hanging above oddly cut narrow canyons with hundred-foot high rock-walls. The further they went the closer they were to Cibola, a rich mountain kingdom with seven great cities of gold. Estevanico, already the first African to enter Texas, was now the first to enter Arizona as well. However, he disappeared shortly after entering the Superstition Mountains and di Niza never set eyes on him again. He assumed that he had been killed by the Zunis. Di

Niza was then warned by his scouts about the natives who were killing anybody who got close to Cibola and that Estevanico had made it there only to be imprisoned and murdered. Di Niza made it just close enough to get a glimpse of what he thought was the legendary lost city before returning back to Mexico to inform Coronado of his disappointing northern mission.

This glimpse was all Coronado needed to convince him to organize an expedition and seize the glory. During the spring of 1540 a large company of men, including di Niza, joined their leader Francisco de Coronado on a journey north in search of the legendary El Dorado. They marched right into northern Arizona and passed through the Superstition Mountains on their way to Cibola. The problem was that they were looking for a city of gold on the outside of the mountains instead of within them. While Coronado's expedition was under way, fellow conquistador Hernando de Alarcon followed with two ships full of goods along the Gulf of California. But he ended up so far ahead of them that he eventually got tired of waiting and decided to keep sailing north; he entered the lower Colorado River, upon which Alarcon and his men came upon the first settlement of the giant Cocopa warriors. Alarcon wisely made peace with these giant American Indians as his ships continued upstream, where they were greeted by thousands more. At the same time Don Rodrigo Maldonado returned from the coast where he had been searching for Alarcon's ships with an American Indian so tall that it impressed Coronado and his fellow Spaniards immensely. Pedro de Castaneda, who accompanied Coronado and later penned the most accurate firsthand account of the expedition, writes:

> Don Rodrigo Maldonado, who was captain of those who went in search of the ships, did not find them, but he brought back with him an Indian so large and tall that the best man in the army reached only to his chest. It was said that other Indians were even taller on the coast.[1]

According to historians this giant American Indian was of the Seri, a great giant tribe that occupied the island of Tiburon and the adjacent Sonora coast on the Gulf of California. In the meantime, Coronado was marching into New Mexico while Captain Melchior Diaz who was still trying to establish contact with Alarcon when he came across more tribes of giant American Indians. Castaneda reports:

> They came to a province of exceedingly tall and strong men—like giants. They are naked and live in large straw cabins built underground like smoke houses, with only the straw roof above ground. They enter these at one end and come out at the other. More than a hundred persons, old and young, sleep in one cabin. When they carry anything, they can take a load of more than three or four hundredweight on their heads. Once when our men wished to fetch a log for the fire, and six men were unable to carry it, one of these Indians is reported to have come and raised it in his arms, put it on his head alone, and carried it very easily.[2]

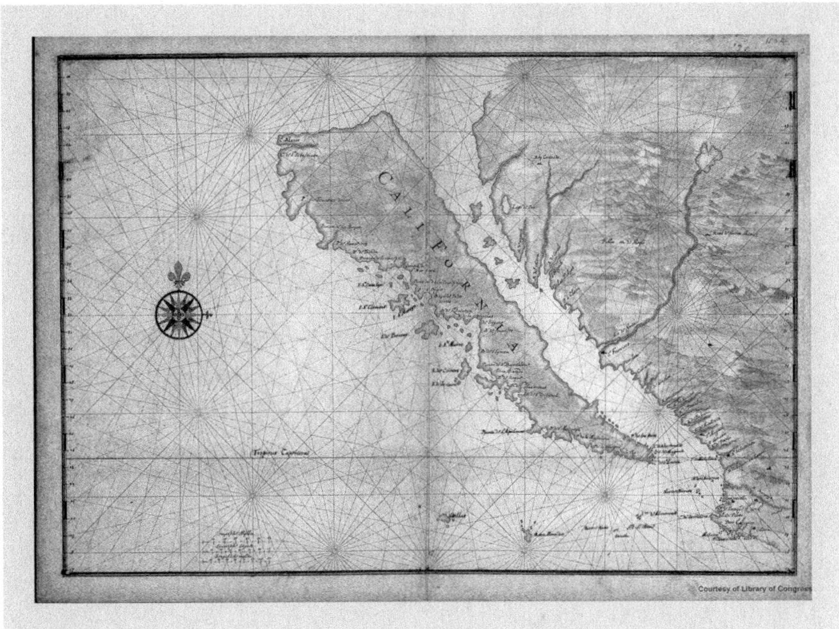

Map of California shown as an island circa 1650.

By the time Coronado got to Cibola he was attacked by a barrage of arrows and forced to retreat with the arrowheads stuck in his armor. Eventually, Coronado and his men stormed the walls of the village and laid waste to the American Indians living there. After a grueling march Coronado and his battered warriors finally entered Cibola and soon feasted on much-needed meals of corn, beans, and turkey. However, while their bellies were full their coffers remained empty. After a lengthy search of the village not a speck of gold or silver was found, and certainly not the fabled El Dorado. Coronado sent expeditions out in different directions while he marched all the way into modern-day Kansas, but each brigade came up empty-handed. By the time Coronado returned to Mexico, more than 80 percent of his platoon had abandoned him. He returned with less than a hundred men, all starving, skinny, and ragged, with no gold to show and no lost city to brag about. His expedition was a disaster. Coronado was branded a failure and removed from his high-ranking position within the Spanish government. Soon after, he died penniless and was almost forgotten about until about 40 years later when Castaneda's book detailing Coronado's expedition was published. In time, Coronado's quest for El Dorado became one of America's great early adventure stories and the Spanish explorers were celebrated for their early achievements in chronicling the strange new history of the Americas. As for the giant Indians they encountered, they, like the rest of their kin, would soon be eradicated and left as a controversial footnote in the history books.

The conquistador quest through Arizona put them in lands that were mystical, dangerous, and ancient, as Wild West pioneers found out a few hundred years later when they began discovering giants buried deep in the desert. Near an area where Coronado and his men marched, railroad workers near Sycamore Creek, Arizona, discovered a prehistoric graveyard of giants as reported by *The New Sentinel* on April 19th, 1926:

> A prehistoric graveyard on Sycamore Creek, where the grade of the Verde railway passes through, has been uncovered by a crew of laborers under the direction of Conductor C.W. Corbin, in performing certain excavations to improve the roadway. There has thus been revealed a very interesting situation that prevailed at some time or another, in the physical make-up of a race is reflected in the massive remains that have been recovered, and which are indisputable of a giant type of humanity that is bewildering to those of this generation. The skull of a human is in the possession of Mr. Corbin together with a portion of the frame that would indicate one who in life must have attained a height of at least 8 feet . . . The bones of the legs likewise are of greater length and heavier than any today.[3]

In 1911, the *Weekly Journal Miner* reported on a giant discovery a few ranchers made when attempting to dig a well in Prescott, Arizona. The ranch owner, Peter Marx, contacted a local attorney and started to make full-scale preparations for a massive excavation before giving the local press a little bit of history about the discovery.

> The bones of this monstrous human may have represented a race of men or a single individual. At any rate, the skeleton of the man in my possession, is sufficiently complete so that the dimensions, which are astounding, may be accurately ascertained and so far as the present generation is to be considered from what I can learn, there is no comparison to be formed. In the first place the skull is of such an abnormal size that if the average man of this day placed it over his head, he still would find room to move it backwards and forwards and up and down with ease, without disturbing his natural position. From measurements taken of this skull, a number 10 hat would be required to fit it. The teeth, several of which are still imbedded in the jawbone, substantiate the immense size of the head. As to the bones, there is no disputing the fact that the owner was symmetrically formed of immense size and herculean strength. The thigh and lower limbs indicate at least twice the size of the average man of today.[4]

Peter Marx also discovered mounds and stone ruins on his ranch near Walnut Creek. He was soon visited by an attaché of the Smithsonian Institution who took pictures of the giant and even offered to buy the mysterious skeleton, but Marx refused to sell. A few months later he mysteriously died in a car accident and no further information emerged as to what happened to the giant skeleton. His land was sold to an unnamed private buyer who quickly barred the public from getting close to the property. In Arizona, near the conquistador-traversed hills of the Superstition Mountains, a giant skeleton was discovered along the foot of the Gila River. The April 19, 1915 edition of the *El Paso Herald* reports:

> "The skeleton of a giant fully eight feet tall has been found near Silver City," said H. E. Davis. The thigh bone of this ancient inhabitant of the southwest measures two inches more than the ordinary man and must have been a giant of great strength. The jaw bone is large enough to fit over the jaw of an ordinary man. A peculiarity of the forehead is that it recedes from the eyes like that of an ape. The similarity is still further found in the sharp bones under the eyes. The skeleton was found encased in baked mud, indicating that encasing the corpse in mud and baking it was the mode of embalming. Near the skeleton was found a stone weighing 12 pounds, which, judging from its shape, must have been a club. The wooden handle has rotted away but there are marks on the stone that indicate that it had been bound to a wooden handle with tongs. It is rather peculiar that less than 30 miles from where this skeleton was found and located on the Gile river are the former houses of a tribe of small cliff dwellers. The existence of these two races so near together forms an interesting topic.[5]

A prehistoric petroglyph image of a giant can be seen on the stone walls of the Rock Art Canyon Ranch in Winslow, Arizona.

A giant on rock art at Canyon Ranch, Winslow, Arizona.

This means that giants were standing on the corner log before Glenn Frey and The Eagles. In neighboring New Mexico a graveyard of giants was unearthed in the winter of 1902. The finding of this ancient giant burial ground caused a sensation in the press as the *New York Times* reported:

> Owing to the discovery of the remains of a race of giants in Guadalupe, N. M., antiquarians and archaeologists are preparing an expedition further to explore that region. This determination is based on the excitement that exists among the people of a scope of country near Mesa Rica, about 200 miles southeast of Las Vegas, where an old burial ground has been discovered that has yielded skeletons of enormous size. Luciana Quintana, on whose ranch the ancient burial plot is located, discovered two stones that bore curious inscriptions and beneath these were found in shallow excavations the bones of a frame that could not have been less than 12 feet in length. The men who opened the grave say the forearm was 4 feet long and that in a well preserved jaw the lower teeth ranged from the size of a hickory nut to that of the largest walnut in size. The chest of the being is reported as having a circumference of seven feet. Quintana, who has uncovered many other burial places, expresses the opinion that perhaps thousands of skeletons of a race of giants long extinct will be found. This supposition is based on the traditions handed down from the early Spanish invasion that have

> detailed knowledge of the existence of a race of giants that inhabited the plains of what now is Eastern New Mexico. Indian legends and carvings also in the same section indicate the existence of such a race.[6]

More reports of this exciting discovery followed like this from the *Albuquerque Daily Citizen* in their January 27, 1902 issue:

> Don Gregorio and Marcelino Martinez have gone down to El Nervo. They will go out to the Mesa Rico and endeavor to buy the skeleton of the human giant which was last week unearthed by Luciano Quintana. The giant would pay if brought here. The Smithsonian people would be proud of a giant of the dimensions of this one. A leg is well preserved. It is eight feet in length. The skeleton will be on exhibition in the court yard and anthropologists are especially invited to examine it.[7]

Luciano Quintana supposedly wired together the giant skeleton and brought it to Las Vegas in the hopes of having it examined and exhibited. However, this is where the trail runs cold and nothing more is ever said about Quintana's giant skeleton.

In the Mormon lands of Utah ancient giants were also reportedly discovered, although some were alleged to have been made up to validate stories contained in their religion's holy book of Mormon. It was a book written in the 1840s that was partly inspired by ancient giants and the mysterious mound builders. One of the allegedly fabricated stories was that of Brewer's cave. In 1955, this cave was supposedly discovered by John Brewer in Manti. According to Brewer, he was led by an ancient stone stairway into a cave that housed a tomb of large coffins containing the mummified remains of an ancient giant race. He also found boxes with metal plates carved with unknown texts inside them. These artifacts were later proven to be fakes and no photos exist of the giants or their tomb. Besides showing the cave to his anthropologist friend, Dr. Robert Heinerman, PhD, who swore to its existence, Brewer never showed anyone else the cave full of mummified giant warriors. Future explorations to find Brewer's cave have since proved useless. However, a Utah giant was indeed discovered near the Jordan River, south of Salt Lake City, as reported by the *New York Sun*, on August 27th, 1891:

> The gigantic skeleton of a man, measuring 8 feet 6 inches in height, was found near the Jordan River just outside Salt Lake City, last week. The find was made by a workman who was digging an irrigation ditch. The skull was uncovered at a depth of eight feet from the surface of the ground and the skeleton was standing bolt upright. The workmen had to dig down nine feet in order to exhume it. The bones were much decayed and crumbled at the slightest touch. They were put together with great care and the skeleton was found to measure 8 feet 6 inches in height: the

> skull measured 11 inches in diameter and the feet 19 inches long. A copper chain, to which was attached three medallions covered with curious hieroglyphics, was found around the neck of the skeleton and near it were found a stone hammer, some pieces of pottery, an arrowhead, and some copper medals. Archaeologists believe that the original owner of the skeleton belonged to the race of mound builders.[8]

It's interesting that this particular giant was buried with a copper chain inscribed with unknown hieroglyphs. Was he a member of that ancient red-headed race of giants or perhaps one of their forefathers from the Prediluvian world? In Blythe, California, a dusty town near the Arizona border, there is a set of amazing geoglyphs on the desert floor. Known as America's Nazca lines, these Blythe intaglios were discovered on November 12, 1931, by Army Air Corps pilot George A. Palmer, who was flying from the Hoover Dam on his way to Los Angeles. Palmer wrote about the imagery of the geoglyphs saying, "Near two of the human shapes are figures of serpents and four-legged animals with long tails. One giant, or god, appears just to have stepped out of a large dance ring."[9] Palmer refers to the image of the giant, and when looked upon from the air and compared to the other surrounding glyphs, it's absolutely certain that whomever made this intaglio meant to emphasize the human's giant stature. Although they are unable to be dated and no records exist of any relatable mythology in the local tribes, historians connect their origins with whomever left the nearby rock art, which is around 2,000 years old. California's southlands are home to some amazing mysteries, including that of a lost city of ancient giants deep in the heart of Death Valley.

In the fall of 1947 Howard E. Hill of Los Angeles, stood before the city's Transportation Club and told a sensational tale about a doctor's discovery of a series of intricate tunnels below Death Valley.[10] But this tunnel system in the heart of the Panamint Mountains was special; it was home to several skeletons of gigantic 9-foot-tall men. Hill's audience was stunned silent as he continued to talk about these giants who were clothed in garments made from the skins of unknown animals. Hill then described the discovery of a ritual hall with strange weapons inscribed with mysterious hieroglyphs and how some areas of the hall were even lined with the bones of ancient saber-tooth tigers and baby mammoths. Hill believed that this underground tunnel kingdom ran an estimated 180 square miles, extending from Death Valley all the way up into the flaming bowels of southern Nevada. However, not one professional archeologist showed up to investigate Hill's claims and the story of the Death Valley giants died a mysterious death. (So too did the discoverers of the cave, as Hill and his two exploring partners vanished after attempting to return to the mysterious underground city of giants). Although inhospitable now, the Death Valley area was once teaming with water, wildlife, and civilization. Ancient petroglyphs and geoglyphs have been discovered there and science has shown that more than 10,000 years ago Death Valley was submerged in water.

One of the giant American Indians that perhaps Coronado and his men might have encountered was dug up and displayed in San Diego near the turn of the 20th century.

Biggest Giant Ever Known: Nine Feet High and Probably a California Indian

> The corpse of the biggest man that ever lived has been dug up near San Diego, California. At all events there is no satisfactory read in ancient or modern history of any human being nearly so tall. The mummy—for in such a condition the remains were found—is that of a person would have been about nine feet high in life. This makes allowances for the shrinkage, which may be pretty closely calculated. As to the accuracy in the estimate there can no question, as the cadaver has been carefully inspected and measured by Prof. Thomas Wilson, Curator of the Department of Prehistoric Anthropology in the Smithsonian Institution, and by other scientists . . . The mummy is that of an Indian and is almost certainly prehistoric, though its age cannot be determined with any sort of accuracy. Historical records of the part of California where it was found go back for at least 250 years, and they make no mention of any man of gigantic stature.[11]

In the summer of 1579, north of San Francisco, English explorer Sir Francis Drake made contact with a tribe of giant American Indians who were so excited to see the navigator that they proclaimed him a god and adorned him with a giant feathered-strewn crown. In his diary, Drake recalled the few days he spent with these Indians while describing them as very tall and possessive of herculean strength. In 1911, the *Oakland Tribune* reported on some of the earliest Indian artifacts found in California; these artifacts once belonged to a giant Indian tribe that lived near the shores where Drake had his encounters with giants 300 years earlier:

> Ethnologists will be interested in a discovery made by Assistant Curator William Altmann of Golden Gate Park Memorial Museum—namely, the fact hitherto denied that the Digger Indians of California were acquainted with at least the rudiments of pottery making. "Until now, no pottery of Digger Indian manufacture has ever been found," says Altmann, and therefore he highly values the find he made in an Indian Burial Mound at Concord, in Contra Costa County. From an excavation made by workmen in the employ of the Port Costa Water Company has been found a large number of Indian relics of great age, including the specimens of crude pottery already mentioned and the skeleton of an Indian giant more than seven feet tall. The skeleton is in the possession of Dr. Neff of Concord, who is mounting it for exhibition.[12]

A few months later readers got an update of the discovery and new details were published:

> The giant skeleton found was 10 feet from the surface and around it were a large number of mortars and pestles, charm stones, and obsidian arrow heads. The giant skeleton has been laid and reconstructed in the

> Curator's office and placed on private exhibition yesterday . . . The skeleton is seven feet four inches. The skull is in great contrast to that of the Indian today. The under-jaw is square and massive, being remarkably thick and strong . . . The find is of the greatest importance to anthropologists the world over, confirming as it does, the theory originally advanced when the giants were unearthed in the Santa Barbara Islands, that a superior race of Indians, both physically and mentally, preceded the Digger and other native races of the present day.[13]

In 1916, while searching for a couple of armed assailants, two Los Angeles lawmen discovered the bones of a giant in a cave above the canyons of Ventura County. The *Los Angeles Times* reported:

> After scouring the various canyons they came upon a wide cavern deep in the brush and hidden from view by a rugged rampart of rocks. Seeing that there was an opening in which the fugitives might take shelter, Mr. Puntenney pulled aside the underbrush and peered into the depths. Within he saw the grinning skull of huge size and the great femur that must have formed the thigh bone of a mighty giant. In this vast and silent region are to be seen ancient ruins that still stand in mute testimony of the fact that at some remote period in the history of our sunny Southland a race of giants lived and moved and had their being . . . The skull, jawbones

> and femur . . . were brought to Moonpark in an office in that town, where examined by Dr. Philo Hull, who has pronounced them unquestionably those of a human being. The bones are being preserved and are on exhibition, they are attracting a great deal of attention.[14]

Unfortunately, these giant bones, much like the rest of the bones in this story, have also gone missing and the trail of their whereabouts ends with the newspaper article. Our final California entry is in tribute to Coronado and his men. It is a discovery that validates Castaneda's claim that the Tiburon Island giants were indeed massive, especially to the short standing conquistadors: "The department of agriculture received yesterday from an agent on Tiburon Island, Gulf of California, the skeleton of a primitive man, more than ten feet tall. It was found a few days ago. Other bones of similar size have been encountered."[15]

Another 10-foot giant was discovered all the way up in the Pacific Northwest, although this one was armed! A cave in Boise, Idaho, caused a worldwide sensation in 1910 when it produced a giant skeleton that defied explanation. A hunting party searching for elk deep in southern Idaho found themselves in an unexplored cave system where they came across the bones of a giant ancient hunter. Next to the giant was a large rusty ancient flint-lock rifle that the discoverers estimated to weigh around 30 pounds. In 1910, the *Sunday Oregonian* reported:

> The skull of this giant is twice as large as that of the average man today. The large limb bones indicate that

Ten-foot-tall skeletons of California. The Washington Times, *July 13, 1908.*

> he must have been a man of great physical power. The skeleton is well preserved and was found upon the surface of the ground far back in the chambers of the cave, stretched out at full length. Close by was the barrel of the rusty rifle, which is of peculiar make unknown to those familiar with firearms. No reasonable theory can be advanced by the discovery as to how the skeleton happened to be in the cave.[16]

In 1912, workmen in Ellensburg, Washington, were dynamiting for excavations when they unearthed the skeleton of a primitive man deep within the glacial drift rock strata. The *Yakima Herald* reported on it.

> Ellensburg, May 11—The skeletons were found 20 feet beneath the surface of the hill, the graves apparently having been tunneled into the hillside. The femur of the largest skeleton is nearly 20 inches long. This, according to Dr. B. J. Moss, would indicate that the man was 80 inches tall, or 6 feet 8 inches, as the man's height is ordinarily four times that of the length of the femur bone. One of the skulls was unusually large, and in the upper jaw has two complete and distinct rows of teeth in front, each set being perfectly formed. This was regarded as decidedly unusual by the normal school professor, who examined the skull closely. He did not regard the two rows of teeth as a racial attribute, but rather as a freak of nature.[17]

In the Belt Mountains of Montana, stories about giant petrified leg bones measuring 8 feet in length along with nearly 10-foot-tall skeletons unearthed by gold hunters have been reported. The tale is pretty remarkable, as it quite possibly describes an encounter with one of the ancient red-headed giants. It also covers the now-familiar territory of giants being discovered in ancient caves with stoned steps leading the way toward vast underground hidden cities full of gold and ancient relics. This was the kind of discovery Coronado was hoping to find.

> A gold hunter said that while prospecting in the Belt Mountains he found a peculiar depression in the ground. After excavating he discovered a mysterious cavern, reached by twenty-three steps. "At the foot of the stairs," said he, "on one side of the passage lay the skeleton of a man of immense stature. The skeleton measured exactly nine feet six inches in height . . . Beside the trunk of the skeleton, I found a copper axe, with an edge harder and keener than any steel instrument of the kind I have ever seen. On the opposite side was a club made of the same metal as the axe. It was shaped not unlike a baseball bat. Under the trunk was a gold plate ten inches long, six inches wide, and one-eighth of an inch thick. It was covered with strange devices."[18]

No further details were published about this amazing discovery and the whereabouts of this ancient cave is unknown. More giant discoveries were made near Pelican Lake, Wisconsin, when two tourists decided to excavate a mound for no other reason than sheer curiosity. After acquiring shovels the pair began digging down to a depth of about 5 feet; they were surprised to find the bones of an 8-foot giant protruding through the earth. Buried with the bones were numerous copper weapons and trinkets along with a necklace made from the tusks of some prehistoric animal. The mighty skeleton was no doubt one of the giants that once roamed the Midwest thousands of years ago. Legends of these ancient giants have been passed down in the mythologies of the Native Americans for hundreds of years, however, these Native histories are in danger of becoming just as extinct as the giants they talk about.

CHAPTER 4

Ancient Giants in Native American Myths and Legends

George Orwell must be rolling in his grave. His account of a future dystopia ruled by an iron-fisted totalitarian elite in *1984* has basically come true in 2016. Orwell's fictional nightmare describes a society in which the government is continually revising history in order to reform it to the desires of the ruling elite. Paradoxically, our society, has evolved into a similar system of rewriting history as it sees fit. What is history, anyways? It's written by the winners. It is a history that befits the elites while they continually suppress the real true story of Earth. It is a history that keeps humanity distracted with wars, money, concerns, and religion. It is a history that forcefully educates society to be ignorant of its own past and the shared history of all human beings.

These ruling elites have managed to maintain control over the academic institutions and the media, allowing very little of unapproved "history" to make it to the mainstream, and certainly not without ridicule and allegations of hoaxing. But there is definitive proof regarding the existence of giants in the form of artifacts and historical accounts, especially in ancient Native American mythologies. Giants in Native American folklore have been described as being anywhere from 20 to 200 feet tall and large enough to capture humans the way a hunter traps rabbits. The following list is a sample of some Native American myths that pertain to giants.

- ***Apache***: The Big Owl was a wicked giant that often played the "bogeyman" role in children's stories. In other Apache tribes, Big Owl was an early opponent of the War Twins and had a significant role as a much-feared mythological villain. The Big Owl giant was described as being a red-headed, man-eating ogre with the ability to shapeshift into a large flying owl capable of snatching up babies and small children.
- ***The Inuit***: The Inuit tribe emerged from western Alaska around 1000 CE and spread east across the Arctic, displacing the older and more mysterious Dorset culture (the Tuniit) in their wake. Inuit legends claim the Tuniit were giants, and much stronger than the Inuit.
- ***The Alsea***: The Asin was a giant cannibal ogress from the mythology of the Alsea tribe. Other neighboring

tribes of the Pacific Northwest like the Salish also had similar myths of monstrous ogres. The giant basket-carrying ogress is common to the folklore of many Northwestern tribes.

- ***The Micmac***: The Chenoos were the evil man-eating giants of northern Algonquin legends.
- ***The Iroquois***: The giants of the Iroquois-speaking tribes were twice the size of normal humans and were supposedly made of stone because their flesh (armor?) couldn't be penetrated by the arrows of even the finest archer. These giants were also cannibals.
- ***The Cree***: The Witiko were the giant cannibals of the Cree. According to Canadian Indian mythology the Witikos were draped in a coat of ice and loved to kidnap children and have them for dinner.
- ***The Navajo***: According to the ancient stories of the Southwestern Navajo tribe, cruel giants once roamed the earth looking for little children to catch and eat.
- ***The Mohegan***: Moshup was a giant warrior revered as a hero of the Mohegan and Wampanoag tribes of the New England area. Moshup was a giant that caught whales with his bare hands and ruled over the people with kindness and mercy, unlike almost all other tales of giants, which portray them as wicked cannibals and ogres.

The Chippewa and Ojibwa also have a mythological story about giants, dogs, and Indians. After their canoe broke in half and they got blown off course, two lost Chippewa natives were captured by a giant who took them back to his earthen lodge:

> An evil Windigo spirit came to the lodge of the giant and told the two men that the giant had other men hidden away in the forest because he like[d] to eat them. The Windigo pretended to be a friend, but he was the one who wanted the men because he was an eater of people. The Windigo became very angry when the giant would not give him the two men, and finally the giant became angry too. He took a big stick and turned over a big bowl with it. A strange animal, which the Indians had never seen before lay on the floor, looking up at them. It looked like a wolf to them, but the giant called the animal "Dog." The giant told him to kill the evil Windigo spirit. The beast sprang to its feet, shook himself, and started to grow, and grow, and grow. The more he shook himself, the more he grew and the fiercer he became. He sprang at the Windigo and killed him; then the dog grew smaller and smaller and crept under the bowl. The giant saw that the Indians were much surprised and pleased with Dog and said that he would give it to them, though it was his pet. He told the men that he would command Dog to take them home. They had no idea how this could be done, though they had seen that the giant was a maker of magic, but they thanked the friendly giant for his great gift.[1]

Tribes in Idaho preserved oral traditions from a time when their ancestors fought with giants along the banks of the Bruneau River. These legendary giants, who made their home near the banks of the river, terrorized the Shoshone for hundreds of years before finally becoming extinct. The present-day natives still refer to central Idaho's Sawtooth Mountains as the Giants House, where in Shoshone legends the Tso'apittse, a rock-armored giant with a cannibal's appetite lives. The legend adds that fire and ice are the only means of killing the giants. Tales such as these have been told and retold for hundreds, perhaps thousands of years in tribal communities. Folklorist memories of giants survived through these narratives, which are still considered factual by many Native Americans; like all myths they have at least a seed of truth within them.

In 1899, Horatio Bardwell Cushman wrote *History of the Choctaw, Chickasaw, and Natchez Indians* in which he describes, "the tradition of the Choctaws . . . told of a race of giants that once inhabited the now State of Tennessee, and with whom their ancestors fought when they arrived in Mississippi in their migration from the west. . . . Their tradition states the Nahullo (race of giants) was of wonderful stature."[2] According to the Choctaw, the Nahullo were a cannibalistic race of white giants that lived near the shores of the Mississippi River. The Comanches, an infamous tribe of the Great Plains, also had mythologies related to the mysterious giants. Chief Rolling Thunder described an ancient race of white giants in 1857:

> Innumerable moons ago, a race of white men, 10 feet high, and far more rich and powerful than any white people now living, here inhabited a large range of country, extending from the rising to the setting sun. Their fortifications crowned the summits of the mountains, protecting their populous cities situated in the

> intervening valleys. They excelled every other nation which was flourished, either before or since, in all manner of cunning handicraft—were brave and warlike—ruling over the land they had wrested from its ancient possessors with a high and haughty hand. Compared with them the palefaces of the present day were pygmies, in both art and arms.[3]

The chief's tale concludes by explaining that when this race of giants continued to maintain their cruel behavior the Great Spirit eradicated them, leaving only their mounds as a testament to their existence. This account was documented by prominent Native American history scholar and researcher Dr. Donald Yates, who also wrote about the Starnake people of Navajo legend, describing them as "A regal race of white giants endowed with mining technology who dominated the West, enslaved lesser tribes, and had strongholds all through the Americas. They were either extinguished or 'went back to the heavens.'"[4]

It is an interesting choice of words. Did they die and go to heaven? Or was he referring to some sort of lost ancient alien technology that allowed them to fly? Perhaps they went back to Paracas with the rest of the red-headed elongated skulled peoples. In Texas, the Karankawa tribes played a pivotal role in early Gulf Coast history, ruling from Galveston Bay to Corpus Christi. This giant nomadic-type culture seasonally migrated between the mainland and the barrier islands stress free until the conquistadors showed up in 1519. The Karankawa were heavily tattooed, pierced, and painted warriors who controlled most of the south Texas islands and even good chunks of

The Gentle Giant from The Lost Giant and Other American Indian Tales Retold, *1918*.

The Gentle Giant.

land 20 miles up into the Rio Grande. They were also cannibalistic in nature and expert hunters possessing a well-deserved reputation of people not to be messed with. In 1768, a Jesuit priest detailed their ritual flesh-eating ceremonies. He described a scene in which the giants would tie their captive to a stake in front of a fire then dance around the victim while dashing in and out, slicing off chunks of flesh. They roasted this flesh in front of the victim and ate it as he slowly died in surreal agony. The Karankawa were impressively tall and wore artful shell ornaments over their bodies, which were greased with shark liver oil to ward off mosquitoes. The origin of the Karankawa tribe is unknown, but some believe they are related to the Seri tribe of "giant Indians," who we discussed earlier as being from Tiburon Island off the coast of California. Seri mythology claims that a race of giants occupied both Baja and coastal Sonora before their arrival. When the conquistadors encountered some of the similar-looking Karankawa on one of the small Texas islands, they said "To this island, we gave the name of Island of Ill Fate. The people on it are tall, and well formed; they have no other weapons than bows and arrows with which they are most dexterous. The men have one of their nipples perforated from side to side and sometimes both; through this hole is thrust a reed as long as two and a half hands and as thick as two fingers."[5]

In 1911, the giant Karankawa were detailed in John R. Swanton's report for the Bureau of Ethnology and described as being "Very tall and well-formed . . . head-flattening and tattooing were practiced to a considerable extent."[6] Unfortunately, the Karankawa, like all other tribes of giant American Indians, fell to extinction due to disease and bloodshed brought on by European conquest.

Another legendary tribe known for being taller than average was the Osage. Plenty of their giant bones were discovered during the ravishing of the mounds of the Ohio Valley during the 1800s and the Osage who survived impressed everyone from acclaimed writers Washington Irving and John Bradbury to legendary explorer Meriwether Lewis and even founding father Thomas Jefferson. On July 12, 1804, after a dozen Osage men visited Jefferson at the White House, Jefferson remarked to Secretary of Treasury Albert Gallatin, "They certainly were the most gigantic men we have ever seen."[7] But the Osage wouldn't be around much longer, and neither would most of their relatives.

When Chief Joseph, the celebrated Nez Perce leader, finally surrendered to the U.S. Army in the Bear Paw mountains of Montana in 1877, he gave a gift to General Nelson Miles (or more like the general confiscated the gift from the chief's medicine bag). The "gift" in question was a spectacular and extremely out of place ancient Mesopotamian 6-inch cuneiform tablet from Iraq. The tablet was translated by Robert Biggs, professor of Assyriology at the Oriental Institute of the University of Chicago and discovered to be a simple sales receipt for a few lambs sold back around 2050 BCE. According to Chief Joseph the tablet once belonged to their ancient giant white ancestors and the relic was passed down among his family for generations.[8] Another Mesopotamian tablet from around the same era was discovered on a farm in Georgia in 1963. This 4-inch tablet, written in the Sumerian language and dated to 2040 BCE, was discovered by a lady digging a flower bed one spring afternoon. The tablet was another receipt that this time recorded the purchase of several goats for a ceremonial sacrifice.[9]

By academia's stubborn acceptance of the independent invention theory, refusing to believe that ancient cultures once traveled freely across the oceans, and that other unknown advanced civilizations existed before the flood, it only continues to hamper their credibility and hinders the seekers of Earth's true history.

As the conquistadors sailed north up the Atlantic coast and into the Carolinas, more tribes of giant American Indians were revealed to them, making it seem as though the northeastern United States was once dominated by a seafaring race of maritime giants.

CHAPTER 5

Giants of the Northeast

IN 1521, PIRATE CONQUISTADOR Pedro de Quejo sailed to the Carolina coast on a secret slaving mission where he accidently discovered a tribe of giant white American Indians. Initially described as European, the Duhare tribe of the Carolinas was affable and unlike any Indian encampment the conquistadors had seen. It's even been speculated by some historians that the Duhare were the leftover survivors from a lost Irish expedition in the 1100s while other scholars maintain the Duhare are from an even older unknown race in the Americas. The Duhare were tall with red to brown hair that hung to the ground, their faces covered with full, lush beards. They made cheese from deer milk, similar to how the ancient Gaelic tribes in Ireland and Scotland did before the English introduced them to dairy cows. The Duhare even had horses, which was strange since the Spanish were supposed to be the ones that introduced the horse to the Americas. Apparently the Duhare didn't receive the memo, as the conquistador Lucas Vazquez de Ayllón subsequently reported that the Duhare owned several horses and had domesticated livestock way before any Spanish conquistadors had shown up.

Datha, the king of Duhare, was described by the Spanish as being a giant, while Datha's wife (the queen) was described as being just as tall as the king. When de Ayllón was dispatched to the Carolinas to investigate this matter of giant white Indians with reddish beards, he got some firsthand experience in strange things. First off, de Ayllón was already familiar with ancient giants, as he allegedly carried around a giant fossilized femur bone as a personal relic. Being a worthy traveler as well, he had lots of experience when it came to identifying native tribes; in regard to the Duhare he clearly noted that they were not Native Americans but white men, possibly European. Second, he stressed the fact that the king and queen were much taller than the average American Indians they ruled over, and instead of a teepee they lived in a rounded stone palace. Perhaps even stranger was that the Duhare seemed to possess an ancient form of pyrotechnic weaponry such as mini-rockets or sparklers. Peter Martyr d'Anghiera recorded de Ayllón's quest in his book *De Orbe Novo*. The reference to sparklers is made during a visit by a shaman.

> When the chief is at death's door and about to give up his soul they send away all witnesses, and then surrounding his bed they perform some secret jugglery which makes him appear to vomit sparks and ashes. It looks like sparks jumping from a bright fire, or those sulphured papers, which people throw into the air to amuse themselves. These sparks, rushing through the

> air and quickly disappearing, look like those shooting stars which people call leaping wild goats. The moment the dying man expires a cloud of those sparks shoots up 3 cubits high with a noise and quickly vanishes. They hail this flame as the dead man's soul, bidding it a last farewell and accompanying its flight with their wailing, tears, and funereal cries, absolutely convinced that it has taken its flight to heaven.[1]

Two hundred years later a German settler was excavating some farm land when he came across more of these mysterious sparklers inside one of the burial mounds of the native Tuscarora of the Carolina interior. *The Colonial Records of North Carolina* describes what happened.

> After the tomb was covered, I noticed something which passes imagination, and which I should not believe, had I not seen it with my own eyes. From the tomb arose a little flaming fire, like a big candle-light, which went up straight in the air, and noiselessly, went straight over the cabin of the deceased widow, and thence further across a big swamp above 1 mile broad, until it finally vanished from sight in the woods. At that sight, I have way to my surprise, and asked what it meant, but the Indians laughed at me, as if I ought to have known that this was no rarity among them. They refused, however, to tell me what it was.[2]

Other giant tribes of the Carolinas were the Chicora and the Tuscarora, who lived near the Duhare and also had legends of giant white men who once lived and wandered in the lands of their forefathers. In his book *Six Nations*, Tuscarora Indian David Cusick wrote that the giants were one of the Great Spirit's original human creations. Some of these giants were reportedly discovered in Wildon, North Carolina, in 1874 when workers broke through a catacomb while digging for a railroad company. The men who found the bodies described the femur bones as long as a full leg of an ordinary man, and the skeletons were at least 8 or 9 feet tall.

In Marion County of West Virginia, an ancient civilization long since vanished left behind artifacts such as earthen forts, burial mounds, petroglyph inscribed stones, and of course giant skeletons. Workers excavating a root cellar in Palatine found two large mummified human skeletons both measuring more than 7 feet tall, but thieves stole the bones the next day; it's rumored that they ended up on the lucrative Indian artifacts touring circuit that existed in the early 19th century. Near Paw Paw Creek at Rivesville, another small former coal mining town in West Virginia, bridge builders smashed into the earth and plowed through sets of heavy clay layers until shockingly unearthing three giant skeletons each with reddish strands of hair. Before the bones deteriorated from being exposed to the air a doctor came in to examine them and ascertained the skeletons to be at least 8 feet tall. While exploring a cave in 1882 amateur archaeologist F.M. Fetty discovered the remains of a giant human sitting with stone and flint artifacts surrounding his prehistoric skeleton. The next summer another giant skeleton was discovered near the same area. This skeleton was almost 8 feet tall as noted by the settlement's nearest doctor, Samuel Kramer of Smithtown.[3]

It seems the lands of Virginia were ripe with these ancient giant skeletons, some of which showcased red hair. Even our nation's greatest founding father, General George Washington, had an encounter with these ancient giants of the northeast. Before he was a revolutionary, Washington was a surveyor for wealthy Virginia landowners. This experience put him on the front lines when it came to building new properties and destroying old ones. In 1754, as a colonel of the Virginia Colonial militia, armed skirmishes had broken out with France, and Washington was ordered to supervise construction of a new fort in Winchester, Virginia. While digging a new foundation workers quickly uncovered a long-forgotten cemetery full of 7-foot-tall skeletons buried around Native American artifacts. Although viewed and reported by Washington, it's not known what happened to the bones after the construction of the fort. Washington's discovery gives credibility to the numerous reports of 7-foot-tall skeletons discovered in the Virginia territories. Even a giant skull with a curious set of teeth was discovered near the Potomac highlands.[4]

Archeologists from the Smithsonian's ethnological division of Eastern Mound studies opened a mound in Iowa that revealed a 7-foot, 6-inch skeleton, as reported by *The Worthington Advance* in 1897:

> It is a matter of official record that in digging through a mound in Iowa the scientists found the skeleton of a giant, who, judging from actual measurement, must have stood seven feet six inches tall when alive. The bones crumbled to dust when exposed to the air.[5]

> In 1933, an eight foot skeleton was discovered by a boy searching for arrowheads in sleepy Steelville, Missouri. From *The Steelville Ledger*, "He turned up the complete skeleton of an 8 foot giant. The grisly find was brought to Dr. R. C. Parker here and stretched out to its enormous length in a hallway of his office where it has since remained the most startling exhibit Steelville has ever had on public view.[6]

Three other reports were published and a photo was taken comparing a 6-foot-tall man with the 8-foot-tall skeleton, which was shipped from Dr. Parker's office to the Smithsonian and never seen again. In addition to these findings, caves in the Ozarks turned up a set of huge, nearly 10-foot-tall skeletons with enormous skulls. Recent trips have been made to rediscover these caves, but numerous floods have made it impossible to locate. Acclaimed newspaper reporter Victor Schoffelmeyer originally reported the discovery in 1913:

> While the historical features of the Ozarks held our attention, by far the most fascinating discovery was one made by an aged recluse and naturalist who for ten years had lived in a shelter cave near where we camped. "Dad" Riggins spent much of his time digging in the ashes which form the floor of many of these caves. At a depth of more than three feet he found the remains of several giant human skeletons, including an almost perfect skull which differed in many particulars from a

> modern specimen. When partly joined the largest skeleton was almost ten feet tall. "Dad" Riggins showed us hieroglyphics covering the Palisades thought to be thousands of years old.[7]

However, the 10-footer was easily outdone by the discovery of an 18-foot skeleton found in West Hickory, Pennsylvania, in 1870. This giant was covered in iron armor, including a monstrous iron helmet corroded with rust. By his side lay a massive 9-foot-long sword. As reported by the *Baltimore American and Commercial* on January 6, 1870:

> While William Thompson, assisted by Robert R. Smith, was engaged in making an excavation near the house of the former, about a half mile north of West Hickory, preparatory to erecting a derrick, they exhumed an enormous helmet of iron which was corroded with rust. Further digging brought to a light sword, which measured 9 feet in length. Curiosity incited them to enlarge the hole, and after a little time they discovered the bones of two enormous feet. Following up the "lead" they had so unexpectedly struck, in few hours' time they had unearthed a well-preserved skeleton of an enormous giant, belong[ing] to a species of the human family which probably inhabited this and other parts of the world at the time of which the Bible speaks, when it says, "and there were giants in those days." The helmet

> is said to be in the shape of those found among the ruins of Nineveh. The bones of the skeleton are remarkably white. The teeth are all in their places and all of them are double and of extraordinary size. These relics have been taken to Tionesta, where they are visited by large numbers of people daily. When his giantship was in the flesh, he must have stood 18 feet in his stockings. These remarkable relics will be forwarded to New York early next week.[8]

Nobody knows whether this story is true, or whether the 18-foot skeleton ever made it to New York, because it has long disappeared from record. Perhaps this giant skeleton was kin to one of the maritime archaic tribes that explored the Northeast more than 7,000 years ago. We've already discussed alternative theories as to the proposed origins of the North American giants. Another possible theory is that the global migrations of the Cro-Magnon during the Maritime Archaic era (7000 BCE to 2000 BCE) was responsible for mixing their dwindling genes with those of the remaining ancient giants that had survived the floods. Archaic-type skulls have sloping foreheads, protruding brows, massive jaws, and extra thick cranial walls. Numerous amounts of these archaic giant-sized skeletal remains have been found in North America. The appearance of these skeletons in the post–Ice Age defies current academic beliefs that each species replaced one another with no interbreeding between them, but it seems the ancient Americas were the breeding grounds to a smorgasbord of mysterious donors.

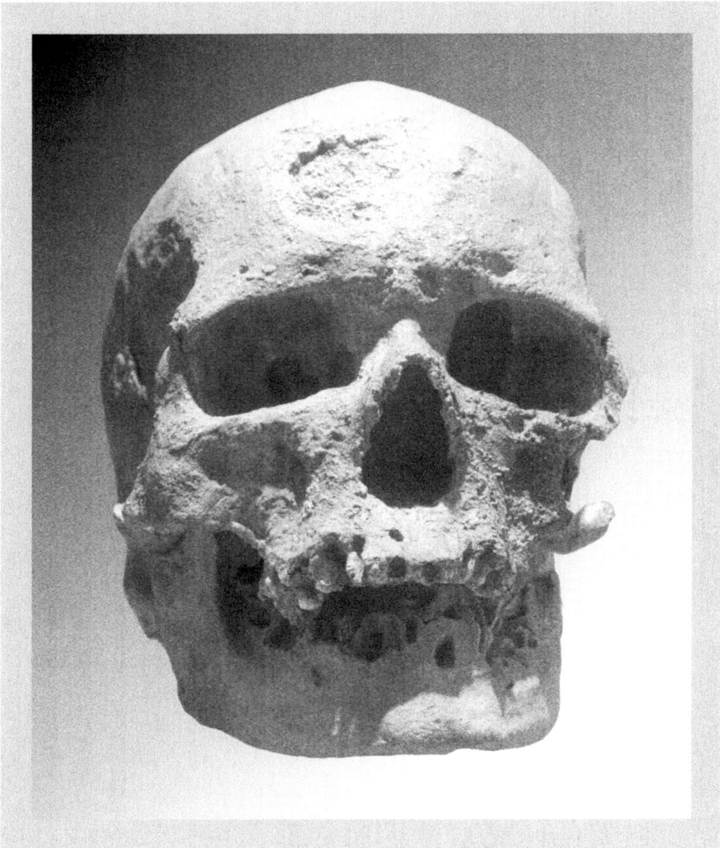

A 35,000-year-old Cro-Magnon skull located at the Musée de l'Homme, Paris.

The *Charleston Daily Mail* published a report on October 22, 1922, proclaiming:

> One of the most interesting of the five state parks is Mound Park, at Moundsville from which that city derived its name. Probably no other relic of pre-historic origin has attracted as wide study among archaeologists as the Grave Creeks mound which has given up skeletons of the ancients who constructed it. . . . Archaeologists investigating the mound some years ago dug out a skeleton said to be that of a female because of the formation of the bones. The skeleton was seven feet four inches tall and the jawbone would easily fit over the face of a man weighing 160 pounds.[9]

Tales of immense giants pervade the indigenous folklore of the Appalachian Mountains. Northern Appalachian lands near Pittsburgh unearthed a 9-foot mummy from a burial mound on a farm in South Huntington Township in 1887 and neighboring Bradford County registered an accurately measured 8-foot, 2-inch skeleton six decades earlier in 1822. In 1878, a giant petrified human head and set of shoulders were discovered at a depth of 75 feet in the same Bradford County area, prompting a quick suppression of their discovery. A giant human molar weighing four ounces was discovered in a Pittsburgh coal bed, more than 600 feet underground, which makes no sense at all considering that coal supposedly formed during the Carboniferous Period, sometime between 286 and 360 million years ago.[10] This means that, giant or no, a tooth shouldn't have been discovered according to the current human historical timeline. The *New York Times* reported on what, at the time, seemed like an important scientific discovery made in Sayre, Pennsylvania, in 1916:

> Professor A. B. Skinner of the American Indian Museum, Professor W. K. Morehead of Phillips Andover Academy, and Dr. George Donahue, Pennsylvania State Historian, who have been conducting researches along the valley of the Susquhanna, have uncovered an Indian mound at Tioga Point, on the upper portion of Queen Earther's Flats, on what is known as the Murray farm, a short distance from Sayre, Penn., which promises rich additions to Indian lore. In the mound uncovered were found bones of sixty-eight men which are believed to have been buried 700 years ago. The average height of these men was seven feet, while many were much taller. Further evidence of their gigantic size [was] found in large celts or axes hewed from stone or buried in the grave. On some of the skulls, two inches above the perfectly formed forehead, were protuberances of bone. Members of the exhibition say that it is the first discovery of its kind on record and a valuable contribution to the history of the early races. The skull and a few bones found in one grave were sent to the American Indian Museum.[11]

Outside of this article, there is no further mention of what happened to the bones or the burials of this mysterious forgotten race. Western Pennsylvania recently unveiled a wood-carved statue honoring one of their most respected Indian chiefs. The intricately designed statue of Chief Wetonah was revealed at Mt. Pisgah County Park with Bradford County officials and a delegation from the Eastern Delaware Nations in attendance. Legend tells us that when Wetonah's bones were reburied for a proper ceremony, a man named Dr. Wilder of Springfield Township measured his skeleton and determined the chief to be at least eight feet tall.[12] Despite this, in 1980, the Army Corps of Engineers decided to build a dam on the sacred area and subsequently wiped out any evidence pertaining to Chief Wetonah's bones or any other giant Indian remains that might have survived. Judge Atlee of York County, Pennsylvania, wrote a fascinating note in his pocket almanac about a giant skeleton his friend witnessed seeing in 1708.

> In company with Chief-Justice Mckean, Judge Bryan . . . and others, on our way to Franklyn, and taking the view of the town in company with Mr. McAlister, and several other reasonable inhabitants, we went to Mr. Neese's tan-yard, where we were shown a place near the currying-house from whence (in digging to sink a tan-vat) some years ago were taken two skeletons of human bodies. They lay close beside each other, and measured about 11 [feet] 3 inches in length; the bones were entire, but on being taken up and exposed to the air they presently crumbled and fell to pieces. Mr. McAllister and some others had seen them, and Mr. McAllister, who is a tall man, about 6 feet 4 inches high, mentioned

> that the principle bone of the leg of one of them, being placed by the side of the leg, reached from his ankle considerable way up his thigh, pointing a small distance below the hip bone.[13]

Even one of America's first folk heroes, Captain John Smith of Jamestown, Virginia, wrote about the giants of the northeastern coast, describing them in his journal as "gyant-like" and saying "those Susquehannocks came to us . . . such great and well-proportioned men are seldom seen, for they seemed like giants to the English."[14] In 1921, flood waters near Berryville, Virginia, unearthed a graveyard of skeletons, each one measuring about 7 feet, 6 inches tall.[15] A 1902 edition of the *Western Virginia Historical Magazine Quarterly* had an interesting letter to the editor that read:

Giant's Axe

> *Charleston, W. Va., March 17, 1902*
> Dear Mr. Laidley: Some years ago when the Colonel Ben Smith mound was opened by Professor Norris, of the Smithsonian, he found the skeleton of a giant which measured seven feet eight inches in length. This occurred about fifteen years ago. Now comes a sequel. A few years ago Joe Foster was ploughing near the mound and unearthed a stone axe. This axe is of granite, beautifully made and well preserved. It weighs seven pounds eight ounces. The largest ever found about here. Dr. J.N. Mahan bought the axe, and has it in his

> possession. Could this have been the giant's axe! Can't you get some of your correspondents to give an article on Indian axes, their history, sizes, &c.![16]

While ploughing land, farmers in Connecticut discovered a forgotten Indian village that was a host to crude copper relics and giant thigh bones more than 20 feet below the surface. Soon, scholars and historians descended upon the site and the discovery made headlines:

> **Skeletons of Stone Age men are dug up in Connecticut—Prehistoric Inhabitants of the Nutmeg Sate Were Flat Heads of Great Strength and Huge Teeth**
>
> *Bridgeport, Conn., August 15*
> Two complete skeletons, supposedly belonging to Stone Age people, were unearthed by a team of archaeologists headed by Professor Warren King Moorehead near the Housatonic River at Laurel Beach. The professor and his assistants had been digging in this section for some time and claimed that the section was once inhabited by a forgotten race based on their findings. Both skeletons are well preserved; the bones are rough, denoting great strength, and the skulls are flat and possess perfect sets of unusually sized teeth. Prof. Moorehead said it was "his belief the bodies were buried in salt water several thousand years ago, which accounts for their preservation.

> He also expressed hope that he and his assistants would soon locate a burial ground of an ancient race."[17]

After an excavation of shell mounds revealed some curious relics in 1916, the *Logan Republican* reported on Professor Norman Wallace Lermond's theories regarding giants that once ruled Maine long before any Europeans showed up:

> Human skulls and bones uncovered in shell mounds at the Pasadena estates by workmen Friday are thought to be the Indian tribe that roamed in this section of the country hundreds of years before America's discovery by white men, is the opinion of Prof. Norman Wallace Lermond, curator and librarian of the Knox Academy of Art and Science, Thomaston, Me., who is wintering here. Lermond, who is also editor of the Maine Naturalist Journal, a monthly periodical, examined the bones in the downtown offices of the Pasadena estates, late Saturday afternoon and in his preliminary inspection volunteered the belief that one of the two skulls in the possession of Jack Taylor was that of a man over eight feet tall. Further examination of the bones will be made by the Maine scientist and he believes that considerable data of importance will be gathered within the next week. The bones were in an excellent state of preservation. They were encased in clay-like receptacles that crumbled at the touch. The skulls however, were solid. The jaws were square and massive, the teeth whole and

> void of cavities. The cheek bones were high. . . . The foreheads were high and not receding as would be expected of age-old human remains.[18]

Gigantic 8-foot-tall skeletons were discovered along the banks of the Choptauk River, Maryland, by members of the Maryland Academy of Science in 1922.[19] The Choptauk takes its name from the tribe of American Indians that lived in this area of Maryland before its settlement by the English. The Choptauk were known to be men of large stature and ruled by the giant chiefs of their tribe. Some of their intact 7-foot-tall skeletons, taken from mounds near Cambridge, can still be seen in the basement of Baltimore's Academy of Natural Sciences. As the crow flies, Baltimore is just 273 kilometers from New York City, an area of mystical lands and near mythical history. New York has always been the center of attraction when people think about America; even back in "ye olden days" New York was an ancient magnet that attracted peoples from all over the globe—especially giants!

In 1904, the *New York Times* reported on a haul of unusual-sized skeletons discovered by railroad workers in Katonah:

> **Katonah, N.Y., Sept. 6.**
>
> While a gang of men in the employ of the New York and Harlem Railroad were taking sand from an immense mound near Purdy's Station to-day to fill in an excavation, they unearthed several skeletons of unusual size. The bones are believed to be those of Indians who once

> lived in this vicinity and belonged to a tribe that was led by the great Chief Teekus, from home the Titicus Valley, now a part of the New York watershed, takes its name. Besides finding the bones, the workmen also exhumed a score or more of arrowheads, hatchets, and copper implements. It is believed that the large mound in which the relics was found were once the burying ground of the Teekus Indians. The last Indians were seen in the valley a short time after the Revolutionary War. The bones found today were brought to Katonah and will be reinterred in the local cemetery.[20]

And hip hop wasn't the only thing to come out of the Bronx; ancient giants supposedly kicked it around Fordham long before any famous rappers did.

Big Skeletons in the Bronx

> Workmen grading Tenth Avenue Extension through the northernmost end of Manhattan Island during the past week have unearthed portions of about a dozen ancient human skeletons in a little knoll about where Two Hundred and Eleventh Street will someday run. Some were nearly complete, but of others only the larger bones remain. They appear to have been interred in an upright position, with the heads about three feet beneath the surface. Bronx Measurements of one skeleton indicates that the man it represents was more than 7

> feet tall. An old cannon ball was found in or near one of the strange graves. Each body rested beneath an uncut stone set endwise. Many similar stones nearby as yet undisturbed indicate that more bones will be found.[21]

Most of the reports we've been exposed to have come from reputable sources such as *The Washington Post* and the *New York Times*, but it was John Wesley Powell, the Smithsonian's director for the Bureau of Ethnology, and a British secret agent who are most responsible for keeping the evidence of giants from reaching the masses on a much broader level.[22] If a report on ancient giants did happen to leak, they made sure there would be no more follow-up articles and the original report would eventually slip into the memory hole. The Smithsonian Institution always seems linked to giant skeletons, especially those that went missing, as most of the turn-of-the-century reports state that the mysterious bones were shipped off to the Institution for further study. More than a hundred years later we know those bones were never seen again and the Smithsonian continues to deny their existence, as it doesn't fit in with their current teaching models of evolution. Although left in the dust during the early stages of scientific discovery, thanks to the pioneers and early explorers of America, the giants have remained in the written record and oral histories of the natives. These stories keep alive the hidden history of a lost race that even stretches toward the frigid lands of Canada, a cold and wooded landscape of mysterious strangers and ancient giants.

CHAPTER 6

Giants of Canada

THE MARITIME ARCHAIC TOOLS found in Canada are at least 5,000 years old and were mainly used for fishing, hunting, or to build boats. These primitive tools were a necessity for the survival of the ancient Maritime Archaic Indians. "Maritime" means they did not farm and relied on the sea for nearly everything, and "Archaic" represents the fact that they were hunters and gatherers on the extreme lower ends of the developmental evolutionary stage. This Maritime Archaic culture fashioned their tools from bones and were associated with the native Indians of northern Canada and its Atlantic Ocean neighbors like Newfoundland and Greenland. They've also been found in Maine and other North American states along the Atlantic coast. Typically distinguished by their long skulls and sloping foreheads this primitive race can also be identified by their gigantic skeletons. This seafaring race can also be found in Northern Scandinavia, Europe, and even all the way into Siberia. In fact, the artifacts of the Maritime Archaic Indians of Canada and the

Northeast American continent are indistinguishable from the artifacts found in the Baltic and Europe. These archaic tools are so similar that even experts can't tell them apart, which reiterates the fact that ancient man was a lover of the seas and had no problem crossing the mighty oceanic highways toward new discoveries.

This explains why, when geneticist Dr. Donald Yates studied the DNA of the ancient Cherokee, he found strong evidence linking them with Middle Eastern ancestry, primarily those of Jewish and Egyptian roots.[1] Clearly ancient humans were not afraid of traversing the oceans. These seafaring adventurers would eventually interbreed and settle in new lands, all the while leaving future mysteries for their descendants to solve thousands of years later. These mysteries include the problematic race of ancient giants, which unsurprisingly can also be found throughout the forested realms of frigid Canada.

A layered burial of more than 200 skeletons was discovered on a Toronto farm in the township of Cayuga in 1880. Most of these skeletons were those of giants measuring more than 9 feet tall. Buried with beads, axes, and stone pipes these giant American Indians preceded the much shorter Mohawks and Ottawa tribes of the Ontario region. Stranger still was the apparent evidence of an ancient city that once existed on this 150-acre Cayuga Township farm. On August 23, 1871, Toronto's *Daily Telegraph* reported:

> There is not the slightest doubt that the remains of a lost city are on this farm. At various times within the past years, the remains of mud houses with their chimneys had been found and there are dozens of pits of a similar

> kind to that just unearthed, though much smaller, in the place which has been discovered before, though the fact has not been made public hitherto. The remains of a blacksmith's shop, containing two tons of charcoal and various implements, were turned up a few months ago. The farm, which consists of 150 acres, has been cultivated for nearly a century and was covered with a thick growth of pine, so that it must have been ages ago since the remains were deposited there. The skulls of the skeletons are of an enormous size and all manner of shapes. . . . The skulls and bones of the giants are fast disappearing, being taken away by curiosity hunters . . . some people profess to believe that the locality of the Fredinburg farm was formerly an Indian burial place, but the enormous stature of the skeletons and the fact that pine trees of centuries growth covered the spot go far to disprove this idea.[2]

On the opposite side of the country, a giant 12-foot-tall skeleton was found on the picturesque Victoria Island of British Colombia. On august 17, 1885, the *New York Times* reported:

> The body of a petrified giant has been found by two farmers who were sinking a well 10 miles from town. Its appearance closely resembles that of a human being. The head has the appearance of having been scalped. The material is as hard as flint and the arms and legs are broken short off. The veins and the ribs are plainly

> traced. A party has gone out for the legs and arms and hands. The man alive must have been about 12 feet in height.[3]

In central Canada near Swan Lake, Manitoba, a 7-foot giant American Indian was found buried with a large axe head measuring more than 16 inches long and 6 inches thick.[4] In Simcoe, Ontario, more than 20 8-foot skeletons were unearthed in ancient burial mounds found on the shores of Lake Erie. In 1872, in western Canada near Comox (which lies over 100 miles northwest of Victoria) excavators plowed through a series of ancient mounds built from blackened beach sands and seashells. These mystery mounds revealed giant skulls, ancient pieces of coal, and eerie stone weapons big enough for hunting mastodons. Or maybe they were hunting ancient giant camels? Natalia Rybcezynski, paleobiologist at the Canadian Museum of Nature, first discovered the bones of ancient giant Ice Age camels on a frosty ridge deep in Canada's High Arctic region in 2013. Later, through a series of DNA tests, they learned the camel's origins stretched back more than 3.5 million years during a time when northern Canada was less chilly and far greener. These giant camels were about 30 percent larger than today's camels, and would have made a perfect traveling companion for Canada's ancient giants.[5] These were the same giants that were found buried in Canadian graveyards and housed away in ancient mounds.

~~~

We have now been exposed to a plethora of information when it comes to ancient giants and strange mounds once existing in North America. These mysteries have sparked an array of questions
~~~

with answers ranging from the improbable to the impossible to the undeniable. However, we have yet to explore the mystical places of Mexico or rummage through the myths of the Maya and the Aztecs. For the lands of the plumed serpent are rich with legends of giants and home to mysterious stone monuments. And as the travel-weary conquistadors made their descent through dangerous jungles, the war drums of natives echoed in the distance, a warning that hunting for gold in the valley of Mexico could have *giant* consequences.

CHAPTER 7

Giants of Mexico

In ancient Mexico, giant beings played a key part in the history and folklore. Their presence is confirmed in the sacred religious and historical texts that survived from the 16th century. These rare texts constructed the ancient history of Mexico as told by the indigenous Indians before their eventual extinction. It is a history that claims giants once lived in Mesoamerica and even helped build the pyramids there. The Codex Rios (Vatican A codex), an Italian translation of ancient Mexican history written during the Spanish conquest by a Dominican friar working in Oaxaca and Puebla, details a lengthy story of Aztec warriors fighting against giant beings.[1]

According to Aztec mythology, some of the Quinametzin (the Old Ones) giants managed to survive the great floods and regrouped to build or rebuild the ancient city of Teotihuacan and the Great Pyramid of Cholula. Teotihuacan was known as the place where men became Gods and it is spread out so that its pyramids and mounds correlate a map of the solar system.

Besides being built by giants, Teotihuacan is associated with other strange anomalies, such as the presence of large quantities of mica.[2] Mica is a mineral that is only found 3,000 miles away in Brazil, but yet somehow managed to make its way to almost every building at Teotihuacan. The ancient Indian, Egyptian, Roman, Chinese, and Greek civilizations were also fans of mica, which contains superior electrical properties as an insulator and a dielectric. Maybe this added mica electrical element was used in conjunction with the hundreds of mysterious, pyrite covered orbs archeologists found buried deep beneath the temple of the feathered serpent. So far, mainstream academia has absolutely no idea what these little yellow balls could have been possibly used for.

The Pyramid of the Sun at Teotihuacan is the largest pyramid in the Americas and second biggest in the entire world. The Maya, Zapotec, and Aztecs all claim that giants built the pyramids found at Teotihuacan. Giant American Indians that were not part of the other Native Mexican tribes still inhabited the lands of Mesoamerica when the conquistadors first arrived in the 16th century, which correlates with the Spanish records that talk about giants everywhere they went in the Western Hemisphere.

According to legends and illustrations contained in the Codex Rios (Codex Vaticano A) giants were still living amongst the Aztecs, although they lived hidden in the jungles and mostly stayed out of the way of the Aztecs. That was until the conquistadors showed up and put everybody's lives in jeopardy. Now, as the conquistadors attempted to overthrow the Aztec stronghold of Teotihuacan, one of the giant warriors known as Tzilacatzin helped fight the Spanish by throwing huge stones down on the

Teotihuacan seen from the Pyramid of the Moon.

Teotihuacan's Pyramid of the Sun.

befuddled conquistadors. Despite being defeated that day the violent Spaniards eventually gained entrance to Teotihuacan and promptly murdered and enslaved the remaining Aztecs, including their giant warrior Tzilacatzi, an American Indian who was most likely related to the Quinametzin giants, who, according to the ancient Mesoamericans, built Teotihuacan.

A son of a Spanish priest, Fray Diego Duran, grew up in central Mexico and was familiar with the remaining giant Indians that stood on the edge of extinction there. Duran was given a unique firsthand opportunity to learn about the Aztecs and the early indigenous history of Mexico. He became a recognized expert on the language, customs, and pre-Columbian history of Mesoamerica and for that reason scholars regard Duran's written works as extremely important. After spending 33 years among the Natives in Mexico, Duran returned to Spain where he wrote a 78-chapter book detailing the history of Mexico from its mysterious origins up until the conquest of the Spanish. When gathering information, Duran conferred with American Indians who knew how to interpret native hieroglyphics into picture-writing manuscripts, helping Duran understand the Native stories and how they related to the accompanying pictographs of hybrid animals and men cloaked in feathered serpent attire. With the help of American Indians, Duran was able to successfully record the ancient history of Mexico, a history that, according to his writings, wasn't shy about the fact that giants once held a formidable presence there. According to Aztec history as recorded by Duran, the lands of central Mexico were ruled completely by a race of giants until local tribes combined forces to run them out of the area. Duran writes that once the tribes had won a few victories and began to settle,

> those from the first region were Chichimecs and the people from Puebla and Cholula were "The Giants," the Quiname, which means "men of great stature." . . . The other people who were found in Tlaxcala and Cholula and Huexotzinco are said to have been "Giants." These were enraged at the coming of the invaders and tried to defend their land . . . of the battles that the Cholultecs fought with the Giants until they killed them or drove them from the country. These Giants lived no less bestially than the Chichimecs, as they had abominable customs and ate raw meat from the hunt. In certain places of that region enormous bones of the Giants have been found, which I myself have seen dug up at the foot of cliffs many times.[3]

Duran's writings offer a valuable glimpse into Aztec history, mythology, and culture, and are among the oldest known Mesoamerican historical texts. The history of Mexico is fascinating and full of fireballs from the heavens, flayed magical serpents, and of course larger than life characters like ancient giants. These giants seem to be everywhere in the history and mythological records of the ancients.

Did the smaller Native Americans walk across the land bridge from Asia while the coastal seafaring giants came over from the South Pacific regions? Were the Denisovans once related to the ancient giants? Did they leave their Neanderthal kin and make their way to the South Pacific where they eventually sailed into Mexico and up near the Caribbean? Does this explain why some tribes of the Solomon Islands have red hair and a natural affection for cannibalism? If these giant Denisovans entered the Americas while landing in Peru and other shorelines in Mexico, it wouldn't be long before their ancient lineage was introduced into the Americas, especially along the coastal areas where their offspring left behind coastal tribes of giants. When the Karankawa traded copper and shells with the red-headed giants of the north, they were likely trading with their own distant relatives, as the Americas was the last settling place of the giants. These were the same giants that, according to the Aztecs, built the round pyramid of Cuicuilco, which mainstream history claims as the oldest in the Americas (discounting that it was built by giants, of course). But when Spanish physician Hernendez entered the odd-shaped pyramid in 1531 he wrote about having found the bones of eerie prehistoric beasts (toxodons and titanotheres) lying next to the bones of men at least 17 feet tall![4]

Another pyramid in ancient Mexico that shares the same architectural style with the pyramids at Teotihuacan (and is located about an hour away) is the pyramid of Cholula. It's no surprise that this pyramid, just like the complex at Teotihuacan, was also built by the Quinametzin giants. When the conquistador Cortes and his men laid eyes on the massive 50-acre structure nearly four centuries ago they were stunned at the architecture, as it was far superior to what they had known back in Spain. The 16th-century Spanish Jesuit missionary Joseph de Acosta shares his personal story of giants in Mexico in *History of the Indies, Volume II.*

> When I was in Mexico, in the year of our Lord one thousand five hundred eighty six, they found one of those giants buried in one of our farms, which we call Jesus del Monte, of whom they brought a tooth to be seen, which (without augmenting) was as big as the fist of a man; and, according to this, all the rest was proportional, which I saw and admired at his deformed greatness.[5]

Fernando de Alba Ixtilxochitl, a native-born Aztec prince and scholar of Mexico in the 1600s, compiled another history of Mesoamerica that proclaimed there were giants in Mexico known as the Quinametzin, who were eventually defeated by the Olmecs and whose bones could be found all over the country.[6] The Spanish priest-historian Juan de Torquemada wrote another chronicle of ancient Mexico, which says that when the Toltecs came to Teotihuacan, "it was inhabited by monstrous giants with long thin arms."[7]

Certain Nahuatl codices even name and depict these giant kings as great builders with godlike abilities. Hubert Howe Bancroft wrote extensively about the history of the Americas in the late 1800s and his epic work on Mayan mythology, the *Popol Vuh*, has become a landmark text of ancient Mesoamerican history. In this highly respected work, Bancroft double-checks all of his historical citations, especially Ixtilxochitl's, and confirms the early Native beliefs that giants once ruled Mexico.

> The Quinames, or giants, are mentioned as the first inhabitants of Mexico. Our knowledge of Olmec

Matthew Stirling and his wife, Marion, with a colossal Olmec head.

> history subsequent to their first appearance is confined to a few events which occurred in Puebla. Here, chiefly on the Rio Atoyae near Puebla de los Angeles, and Cholula they found the Quinames, or giants. These Quinames, as Ixtlilxochitl states, were survivors of the great destruction which closed the second age of the world. The Quinames, traditionally assigned as the first inhabitants of nearly every part of the country, have been the subject of much discussion among the Spanish writers. Clavegero considers the existence of a race of giants doubtful, although admitting that there were doubtless individuals of great size among them. Villa Senor y Sanchez, one of the early Spanish writers, names Tula as one of the many localities where giants' bones had been found. . . . Humboldt mentions some giants' bones that were found within the limits of the state of Michoacan. Ribas, in his standard and very rare work on "The Triumphs of the Faith," says: "At San Agustin, between the city of Durango and San Juan del Rio, Arlegui notes the existence of bones of giants."[8]

Bernal Diaz del Castillo, a soldier during the Cortes conquest of the Aztecs became friendly with the Tlaxcatecs, who told him that a race of giants had once inhabited their land. Castillo later wrote a captivating book called *The Conquest of New Spain from the Cortes Expedition to Mexico Around 1520*, which stirred imaginations for

The Storming of the Teocalli by Cortez and his troops.

centuries. In it, Castillo shares his story about that enigmatic race of Mesoamerican giants.

> They said their ancestors had told them that very tall men and women with huge bones had once dwelt among them but because they were a very bad people with wicked customs they had fought against them and killed them, and those of them who remained had died off. And to show us how big these giants had been they brought us the leg-bone of one, which was very thick and the height of an ordinary-sized man, and that was a leg-bone from the hip to the knee. I measured myself against it, and it was as tall as I am, though I am of a reasonable height. They brought other pieces of bone of the same kind, but they were all rotten and eaten away by the soil. We were all astonished by the sight of these bones and felt certain there must have been giants in that land.[9]

Acclaimed historian Bernardino de Sahagun arrived in the Americas in 1523 and later wrote a 12-volume tome on pre-conquest Aztec history, backing up the claims that the Quinametzin were ancient giants that built both the Teotihuacan and Cholula pyramid complexes. Sahagun also chronicled the strange paranormal activity associated with the pyramids, as 10 years prior to the conquest, a great triangular ball of flame hovered in the skies for one year straight, causing much concern among the tribes. More weird things followed, including fires of unknown origins and rays from the skies that leveled some of their temples and pyramids. These events were seen as omens and that a great change was coming, and it did with the arrival of "comets in the heavens flying in threes"[10] that left behind strange heavy sounds and waves of vibrations in their wake. This period of extreme Aztec uncertainty produced more outlandish niceties; Sahagun writes of a monstrous winged bird brought before a disturbed Moctezuma. This bird even had a magical "mirror" on its head that dazzled Moctezuma's astrologers with visions of marching armed soldiers riding strange beasts. Was this "mirror" some sort of television monitor and were these beasts actually horses? After all, horses *were* actually strange beasts that American Indians had never seen before the arrival of the Spanish. Whatever this mysterious bird was, it vanished before Moctezuma's eyes, signaling that the world as they knew it would soon be coming to an end.

It wouldn't be long before old empires fell and new kingdoms were built, and with it so goes the histories of the fallen, rewritten to the befitting of future historians. And although both the ancient Aztecs and the conquistadors spoke of a race of long-forgotten giants that still remained in dwindling numbers, the history books have succeed in editing out this bit of fascinating history.

Hundreds of years after the Spanish had settled Mexico, farmers, engineers, and workers were once again digging up and discovering giant bones while either ploughing their fields or digging construction on new buildings. In 1909, builders near Mexico City, the original stomping grounds of the Quinametzin giants, found a 15-foot-tall skeleton. As reported in the February 3, 1909 edition of the *New York Tribune*:

Ancient giant as depicted by the Aztecs.

Find Prehistoric Giant
Skeleton 15 Feet High Unearthed in Mexico

News was received here Monday from Mexico that at Ixtapalapa, a town 10 miles southeast of Mexico City, there had been discovered what was believed to be the skeleton of a prehistoric giant of extraordinary size. A peon while excavating for the foundation of a house on the estate of Augustin Juarez found the skeleton of a human being that is estimated to have been about 15 feet high, and who must have lived ages ago, judging from the ossified state of the bones. Romulo Luna, judge of the District, has taken possession of the skeleton which is complete with the exception of the skull. Judge Luna says that as soon as the search for the skull is finished the skeleton will be forwarded to the national museum, of Mexico, which has an almost priceless collection of Aztec antiquities. The National museum, it is said, has made arrangements to investigate this "find." The discovery of the skeleton has revived the old Aztec legend that in a prehistoric age a race of giants lived in the valley of Anahuac, a name given by the aboriginal Mexicans to that part of the Mexican plateau nearly corresponding to the modern valley of Mexico City. These giants, known as Quinatzins, the story goes, were afterwards destroyed by the Ulmecas, also of great stature, who in turn, perished by earthquake, interpreted as an expression of the wrath of God.[11]

Near the Arizona border, the lands of Sonora, Mexico, provide plenty of ancient giant mysteries from history to chew on. In 1930, the *New York Times* reports:

> Tuscon, Ariz., Dec. 1 (AP) Discovery of apparent remains of a race of giants has been made at Sayopa, Sonara, a mining town 300 miles south of the Mexican border. J.E. Coker, a mining engineer, reports that laborers clearing ranch land near the Yaqui River dug into an old cemetery where bodies of men, averaging eight feet in height, were buried tier on tier. The heads of the skeletons, Coker said, were especially large. Carved native stone bracelets were found on the bones. Beside the bodies, the crudest kind of stone weapons and implements were buried. After the first skeleton was unearthed owners of the ranch redoubled efforts to excavate in the cemetery.[12]

No follow-ups exist for either of the previous stories, but it would be curious to learn what happened to the giant 15-foot-tall bones that we assume ended up at the National Museum of Mexico. Once again the verifiable mind-blowing physical evidence, such as the ancient giant robes and blonde-haired skulls discovered by the explorer Paxson Hayes in northern Mexico's Copper Canyon, alludes us. This amazing story is almost too good to be true, but it does fit into the proper locations (caves) and overall strangeness associated with the lost race of giants. The odd thing in Paxson's case is the fact that the hair discovered on the giant skulls was blonde instead of red. Hayes, a herpetologist, had heard legends about the ancient blonde giants from the local Sonora Indians and decided to investigate the tales further while searching for rare snakes in the high desert canyons. About his startling discovery Hayes said:

> "Every basket we found contained a body wrapped like a silkworm. There were 34, of which two were women. Nine were mummified and the remainder were skeletons." When the bones of the mummies were laid out properly the various bodies measured from 7 feet, 6 inches in most cases up to the largest skeleton which was a full eight feet! . . . The greatest mystery of Hayes' find, and perhaps the key that one day may solve this riddle of the Mongoloid past, were the saffron colored burial robes found on the giants. There may be a great historical tale behind the powder-blue designs of latch hooks and pyramids that embellish the robes. Hayes thinks that the tiny series of white dots that recur throughout the robes are symbols of the ancient Indian time cycle, and, working on that theory points out that if this be true . . . . The white dots add up to 25,000 years. He took the burial robes to the chiefs of the Seri Indians on Tiburon Island off the Mexican west coast. They were as puzzled as Hayes.[13]

Paxson Hayes even brought his findings to the Seri Indians, who were related in some way to the ancient giants, and they didn't even know what they were looking at! More follow-ups were made into the Hayes discovery and even a few photos were published of the giant skull and the robe: "Paxson Hayes, explorer, studies the head of a giant mummy discovered by him in a deep cave hitherto unexplored regions of Sonora, Mexico. The mummified remains were of a race 7 1/2 feet tall and preserved in excellent condition. Corn found with the mummies has been given to scientists."[14] A year later Hayes took his discoveries on the road with him and impressed folks all across America up until his arrival at the Smithsonian. The July 22, 1937 edition of the *Washington Post* reported:

> With several dozen snakes (all alive), and the burial robe of a prehistoric giant (quite dead), packed in their trailer, they stopped in Washington yesterday to promote interest in their unique fields of activity. Herpetologically speaking, their purpose in coming here from California was to present President Roosevelt with 15 Smoki snakes, 10 California and Mexican rattlers and an 8-foot baby Mexican boa constrictor, which was shedding. Marvin C. McIntyre received them at the White House, expressed gratitude and suggested the reptile house at the zoo as perhaps the best place for the snakes. Dr. Ernest P. Walker, assistant director of the zoo, officially welcomed the snakes to their new home. That over, the visitors then dropped in at the Smithsonian Institution with the prehistoric burial robe and a four-legged stool, both of which they unearthed in a burial cave in northern Sonora, Mexico.

> The Californians explained that the cave, one of 18 they had discovered, contains well preserved mummies of a race which averaged over 6 1/2 feet in height (up to 8 feet tall). The caves are scattered over an area of 450 square miles. Hayes who has just returned from his fifth expedition to the caves heard about their existence from the Yaqui Indians of Mexico.[15]

The *Annual Report of the Board of Regents of the Smithsonian Institution* confirms that Hayes met with Smithsonian officials and gave them the burial robe from a lost race of giants.[16] As usual, it became another thing associated with giants that ended up lost after a visit to Washington. Hayes also claimed that he found more giant skeletons in New Mexico, although these giants were much different looking and considered by Hayes to be of Asian origins. However, unlike the Copper Canyon discoveries, Hayes chose not to provide evidence of his findings, perhaps bitter that the Smithsonian hadn't been returning his calls. So here we have a rediscovered fabled lost city, a giant mummified head, and a burial robe of a giant, all three with accompanying photographs published in the most prestigious newspapers of the time, yet nearly 20 years after his initial discovery Hayes still couldn't get a proper scientific investigation to validate his claims. More than 60 years later, Hayes, his findings, and his mysterious legacy have all but vanished without a trace.

Back in central Mexico 8-foot giant Indian skeletons were still being unearthed and reported on by the *New York Times* in, for example, this article from 1925:

Cave in Mexico Gives Up the Bones of an Ancient Race

> Boston, May 3—Charles C. Clapp, who has recently returned from Mexico, where he has been in charge of Thomas W. Lawson's mining interests, has called the attention of professor Agasaiz to a remarkable discovery made by him. He found in Mexico a cave containing some 200 skeletons of men each above eight feet in height. The cave was evidently a burial place of a race of giants who antedated the Aztecs. Mr. Clapp arranged the bones of one of the skeletons and found the total length to be 8 feet 11 inches. The femur reached up to his thigh, and molars were big enough to crack a cocoanut. The head measured eighteen inches from front to back.[17]

During the settling of Mexico, numerous reports of giant skeletons ranging from 7 to more than 13 feet in height can be found. There's even the curious case of the sub-genre species of giants that have six toes and fingers; ancient hieroglyphs in Mexico even depict them. Chronicles 20:6 tells us about the ancient six-fingered giants of the Holy Lands: "And there was again war at Gath, where was a man of great stature, whose fingers and toes were four and twenty, six [on each hand], and six [on each foot]; and he also was born unto the giant.[18]

Even the ancient giant Goliath was noted to have six fingers, but we'll talk more about these giants in a following chapter. To the ancient Mexicans the belief in giants was a foregone conclusion. It was an unmistakable fabric of their origins, woven into their ancestry without the slightest bit of condescendence. The mythological history of Mesoamerica, along with the region's impressive pyramids and archeological discoveries of large bones, both past and present, proves that ancient Mexico was once home to that mysterious race of lost giants. This giant kingdom stretched from the jungles of Mexico to the warm waters of the Caribbean, where the infamous conquistador Amerigo Vespucci was about to discover an island full of them.

CHAPTER 8

Vespucci and the Giants of the Caribbean

No book about giants of the Americas would be complete without mentioning Amerigo Vespucci, the man for whom one-third of the world is named after. But why was most of the Western Hemisphere named after him? Is it because America (named by a German geographer in 1507) has a better ring to it than the United States of Columbus? No, it's because Vespucci realized the lands he was exploring were two separate continents and not a part of Asia (or India as he and most others believed at the time). Although if the German geographer hadn't published a paper proclaiming why it should be named in honor of Vespucci, who knows what the continent would have been called.

Vespucci was an Italian merchant, born in 1454 in Florence to wealthy parents. He grew up around and was later employed by the Medicis, the mega-rich banking family that basically owned northern Italy. Vespucci was sent to look after their ship-outfitting business in Seville, and even had a hand in outfitting Columbus's third voyage, an event that inspired Vespucci's own quest to search for that elusive passage to India. In 1499, seven years after Columbus first landed in the West Indies, Vespucci departed Seville on his maiden voyage across the ocean. During this first voyage he crossed the Atlantic and landed on the northern coast of South America. He glimpsed the mouth of the Amazon and made journeys inland around the fringes of Southern Brazil. His first views of giant natives came while looking for water on the outskirts of the Brazilian jungles but the big breakthrough came on Vespucci's second journey of expedition.

After exploring the coasts of Venezuela, Vespucci and his ship floated toward the tiny Caribbean island of what is now Curacao. The story unfolds in the *Second Voyage of Amerigo Vespucci* translated from the original text by Oxford scholar Clements R. Markham in 1893.

> We found that this other island was inhabited by very tall people. We landed to see whether there was any fresh water, and not thinking it was inhabited, as we had not seen anyone, we came upon very large footprints in the sand, as we were walking along the beach. We judged that if the other measurements were in proportion to those of their feet, they must be very tall. . . . When we had gone about a league we saw five huts, which appeared to be uninhabited, in a valley, and we went to them. But we only found five women, two old, and three children of such lofty stature that, for the wonder of the thing, we wanted to keep them. . . .

> While we were forming this design there entered by the door of the hut as many as thirty-six men, much bigger than the women, and so well made that it was a rare thing to behold them. . . . They carried very large bows and arrows, and great clubs with knobs. They talked among themselves in a tone as if they wished to destroy us. . . . We called this island, the Island of the Giants, by reason of their stature.[1]

Vespucci's tale is an extremely fascinating account of 16th-century island hopping! Conquistador Alonso de Ojeda, a fellow explorer, discovered and named another "Island of Giants," this time on the neighboring island of Aruba, although in time the name would be changed to "useless island," as the Spanish found no gold or anything of value there. Historians have argued whether or not they are both talking about the same island, but considering that both islands are within close proximity of each other, it's possible both had tribes of native giants ruling over their earthly paradises. The giants they managed to enslave were deported to work in Hispaniola where they soon died while out mining for gold.

The Spanish colony established in Santo Domingo in 1496 soon became their headquarters for gold hunting in the Caribbean. They set up mines and enslaved the local Arawak-Lucayan Indians they found living there. In the early 1500s the conquistadors were roaming around the Caribbean islands searching for gold and silver and enslaving or killing any Indian who resisted. By the time they had set up shop in Cuba they had reduced the most feared tribes of the Caribbean to the edge of extinction. The original inhabitants of the main Caribbean islands of Cuba, Hispaniola, Jamaica, Puerto Rico, and the Bahamas were the Arawak, the Lucayan, and the Taino Indians, who were all described as being tall statuesque people with long black hair. When Columbus arrived in the Bahamas in 1492 he encountered the Lucayan and was impressed by their canoes, ceramic art, and appearance, but eventually deemed them expendable since they had no gold.

When Columbus and his crew arrived, the Lucayans first mistook them as returning gods, because according to their oral history, the gods used to fly around in the skies and promised one day to return. Columbus even noted in his journals the strange presence of mysterious orange-colored flying orbs before making landfall in Cuba. However, Columbus wasn't flying a spaceship, and although he was dressed mysteriously and harboring huge vessels with unknown technology, the Lucayans quickly discovered he was no god. The interesting thing about the Lucayans in relation to flying ships and ancient aliens was the fact that they practiced the cranial deformation and head-flattening techniques used to produce elongated skulls. This meant that, at some point in their history, what the Lucayan were saying about gods, or something they interpreted as gods, flying around in the Caribbean might have been true, as they maintained the practice of cranial deformation to imitate and honor these so-called gods. The Taino and the Arawak also shared this practice.

Based on petroglyphs found in the Dominican Republic's Pomier Caves, indigenous tribes like the Taino have been documenting Caribbean history for thousands of years. The Pomier Caves are a thousand feet below sea level and contain more than

Pictograph in Pomier Cave 1.

5,000 pictographs of animals, humans, giants, and mysterious alien-looking beings with elongated heads. But the ancient giants that once wandered the Caribbean did so at a time when the waters were much lower. Science has shown that before the end of the last Ice Age (12,000 years ago) ocean levels were at least 400 feet below their current levels. This meant that the Bahamas and Cuba were all part of one vast island in the remote past instead of the chain of islands they are today. America's greatest prophet, Edgar Cayce, believed that the remnants of Atlantis would be found between the Bahamas and Cuba, and referred to Bimini as the ancient mountaintop of Atlantis. The strange rows of stone roadways, cylinder columns, and marble ruins appearing in Bimini have left historians scratching their heads in wonder for decades.

Catastrophic earthquakes and untold amounts of hurricanes have concealed the ruins of Atlantis for thousands of years, but the discovery of what appears to be a megalithic wall was discovered in the shallow waters near Bimini in 2007. According to locals, "Joulter's Wall"[2] is a huge underwater wall located in the shallow waters of Joulters Cays, about 5 miles north of Andros Island. The cays and accompanying island are completely uninhabited, and the extremely shallow waters that surround it make it hard for boats to reach, but expert divers like Dr. Greg Little and his wife, Lora, have made the attempts to document the mysterious walls. Capturing a series of amazing photographs that seem to prove the authenticity of the walls' antiquity, they even noted the presence of tool marks on the walls. However, it's impossible to tell whether the walls are old enough to be considered part of Atlantis or whether they are much more modern, perhaps built by the Phoenicians or even the giant ancestors of the Arawak.

In the late 1990s a joint Russian-Canadian expedition was helmed by oceanographic engineer Paulina Zelitsky, who used high-tech equipment and underwater cameras to find and film a series of mysterious structures off the coast of Cuba. Sending probes down more than 2,200 feet Zelitsky was able to film images of what appeared to be pyramids, plazas, and terraces, which looked similar to the ruins of Teotihuacan. This shocking discovery of a lost city sleeping off the coast of Cuba was reported on briefly by the BBce in the winter of 2002 and was mentioned in a short article about Caribbean flood myths in the November issue of *National Geographic* magazine.[3] Then it was never talked about again by the mainstream media. It is obvious to see why, as it challenges their timeline of history. As the giant Indians of the Caribbean were systematically wiped out shortly after the arrival of the Spanish, most of their history and proof of their lineage went with them. Very little information about the giants of the Caribbean has survived, and the same goes for the Ice Age and Atlantean-type civilizations. But there's a whole other continent that lies on the outer reaches of the warm Caribbean seas: South America, a land rich in ancient mysteries, megalithic wonders, and giants.

CHAPTER 9

Magellan's Magical Mystery Tour and the Giants of South America

The Spanish conquistadors were among the first to explore the mystical lands of Patagonia, where, along the coast of what is now southern Argentina, they first viewed giants of mythical proportions. These Patagonian giants, like other tales of exotic characters in far-off places, captured the imaginations of Europeans for hundreds of years. This mythical race of giants first surfaced in the 1520s from the writings of Antonio Pigafetta, the Venetian scholar who was ordered to accompany Magellan on the orders of King Charles I of Spain. Magellan used Italian explorer John Cabot's maps, which led him along the coast of Brazil and eventually to the country we presently call Argentina. While wintering in an Argentine harbor near the artic at the bottom of South America, Magellan and his crew had their first encounter with the Patagonian giants. Pigafetta writes:

> But one day (without anyone expecting it) we saw a giant who was on the shore [near today's Puerto San Julián, Argentina], quite naked, and who danced, leaped, and sang, and while he sang he threw sand and dust on his head. Our captain [Magellan] sent one of his men toward him, charging him to leap and sing like the other in order to reassure him and to show him friendship. Which he did. Immediately the man of the ship, dancing, led this giant to a small island where the captain awaited him. And when he was before us, he began to marvel and to be afraid, and he raised one finger upward, believing that we came from heaven. And he was so tall that the tallest of us only came up to his waist.[1]

Again this is another curious question of whether or not they had come from the skies. Why would they keep asking this question if at some point in ancient history they weren't witness to things flying around in the sky? It took Magellan and eight other men to seize the two younger giants in an effort to bring them back to Spain, but the giants died within weeks of being chained to the bottom decks of a ship. Magellan didn't make it back to Spain either, as he died after being shot by a poisonous arrow in the Philippines. Pigafetta, the chronicler of the expedition, was one of only 18 men who survived Magellan's journey around the world.

Five years later another Spaniard, García Jofre de Loayza, also reached Patagonia and had his own encounters with these giants. Juan de Areízaga, a priest who was part of the expedition, recorded in his journals that some of the native men were more than 9 feet tall. Fifty years later, Sir Francis Drake followed the same route as he guided a fleet of five ships down the coastline of South America. Drake was the legendary English admiral who helped defeat the Spanish Armada, earning a knighthood from Queen Elizabeth I. He was also a slave trader and pirate with a deep hatred of Spain, barely escaping death from the clutches of the conquistadors more than once. Drake wasn't a very popular captain either; during the trek toward Patagonia rumors of a mutiny were swirling, so Drake docked off the coast of Argentina for a quick kangaroo court where he found the accused guilty and quickly beheaded him. Drake then led the fleet into the Strait of Magellan and on to the Pacific Ocean where they got caught in a massive storm. Drake soon lost the rest of his fleet but continued on in the only remaining vessel from the journey. In it he sailed up the coasts of Peru and Chile raiding and plundering unprotected Spanish ships on his way across the Pacific Ocean and back.

Meanwhile, Drake's cousin was battling against indigenous giants in Peru after being shipwrecked and separated from the expedition during the storm. John Drake departed with first cousin Sir Francis as a bright-eyed 15-year-old eager for adventure, but wound up captured by the Spanish and suffered an early death at the tender age of 23. It was a hard eight years in the New World for John, who spilled his guts about his giant encounters while being interrogated by the Inquisition in Lima, Perú, in 1587. Three years later, Sir Francis Drake ceremoniously returned to Plymouth where he was hailed as the first Englishman to circumnavigate the world. This quest confirmed the reports of indigenous giants in Patagonia as first documented by the Spanish conquistadors. In *The World*

English sailor offering bread to a Patagonian woman giant.

Encompassed, Sir Francis Drake's ship chaplain, Francis Fletcher, wrote about the giants of Patagonia.

> They found the print of the feet in the soft ground, the breadth whereof was the length of one of our men's feet of largest size, which could be no other than the foot of a giant, so that we conjectured that the giants did possess some part of Brasilia on the North side of the river of Plate. . . . We thus coasting along, perceived that the main land from the river of Plate to the Strait of Magellan is wholly inhabited of the giants . . . for we touched with no land anywhere along that land where we met not with them in great numbers. . . . And here with the General . . . went on shore, where the giant men and women with their children repaired to them, showing themselves not only harmless but also most ready to do us any good and pleasure because they never knew what a man meant before for no people ever frequenting those parts, but only the giants the inhabitants, they were never beaten or disquieted to breed in them any dislike, for the giants themselves never use boats or come upon the water, nor so much as touch water with their feet, if they can by any means avoid it. . . . Now as we have spoken of the men giants, so it is not amiss we speak somewhat of their women. First, then, afore as the men in height and greatness are so extraordinary that they hold no comparison with

> any of the sons of men this day in the world, so the women are answerable to them in stature and proportion every way and as the men never cut their hair, so the women are ever shorn, or rather shaven, with a razor of a flint stone, whereof they make all their edged tools and cut one of them with another—we could not perceive that this people had any set government.[2]

Later, they landed in Port Saint Julian, another port in Patagonia where, after docking on the south side of the harbor and taking time to freshen up, they met more indigenous giants.

> When we had refreshed our men, the General with chosen men went on shore, to see what the place might afford us for our maintenance, if we should make any stay. Who no sooner landed but two young giants repaired to them, shewing themselves at the first as familiar as any we had met with before, insomuch they refused nothing which was offered to them at the first sight but the thing wherein they most pleased themselves was to see to shoot an arrow out of our bows farther at one shot than they could at twice. They thus familiarly and pleasantly spending their time, suddenly there came two other giants (old and grim weather beaten villains) . . . for they sent away the two younger giants with dislike that they had been in our company.[3]

After becoming low on food Magellan sent hunting parties to search the cold tundra of Patagonia for provisions, but the most they could find were mussels, seaweed, and bird eggs (the ostrich eggs were preferred by the giants).

> We were driven to search corners very narrowly for some refreshing, but the best we could find was shells instead of meat, we found the nests but the birds were gone, that is, the shells of cockles upon the banks of the shore where the giants had banqueted . . . The shells was so extraordinary that it will be incredible to the most part, for a pair of shells did weigh four pounds, and what the meat of such two shells might be may easily be conjectured. I make account it weighed one pound at least, so that it was a reasonable bit for a giant.[4]

Artic explorer and physician Dr. Frederick Cook seemed to verify these giants by identifying the primary tribe as the Ona, the last surviving giants of Patagonia. Cook encountered them during his "Belgica" expedition in 1896, noting how they lived simply in wigwam huts and dressed in animal furs to keep warm. His photographs of the giant Ona offer us undeniable proof that the lineage of a lost giant race did indeed exist. The average height of the Ona ranged from 6 1/2 to 8 feet tall; there's even a photograph archived in the Library of Congress listing one of the Ona as 7 feet, 4 inches in height. Charles Darwin described the Ona and their neighboring tribes like the Fuegians as cannibals.

The fact that these giants practiced cannibalism relates them to the other giant cannibal prone tribes found throughout the Americas. On July 30, 1899, *The San Francisco Call* ran the story about Dr. Cook's giant Indian encounters deep in the frigid lowlands of artic Argentina.

Biggest Race of Men in the World

> Dr. Frederick A. Cook, who has just returned from an exploring expedition to the South Polar regions, brings photographs of a race of cannibal giants discovered by him near the Antarctic Circle. The existence of such a race has always been denied by scientists, but Dr. Cook has not only seen and talked with them, but brings back photographs to prove beyond argument that the biggest race of human beings in the world is to be found in the frozen south. The monstrous forms of both the men and women are clad in furs; the men arm themselves with bows and arrows and wooden clubs. Their strength and endurance are remarkable. The men can outrun any horse on a long stretch. They can cover fifty miles in a few hours. They live in the Antarctic regions and have just been discovered by Explorer Cook.[6]

Anthropologists documented seeing the last remaining giants of Brazil in the 1970s and no further information regarding their whereabouts exists. But the mysterious human genepool keeps getting older and more complicated, as scientists recently announced the discovery of a Neanderthal toe bone containing human DNA. This pushes back the intermingling of the species to at least 110,000 years ago according to forensic science experts.[7]

Back in 1579, Drake's voyage of discovery was troubling the Spaniards, who sent mercenary Pedro Sarmiento de Gamboa to cut off and capture Drake at the Strait of Magellan. The Spanish hoped to remain the sole ruling force in the Americas and wanted to avoid any possible future English occupation in the region. But Gamboa missed Drake and ended up running into the Patagonia giants instead. In his written account he tells us that the natives were "Giants"[8] and that was because of their tremendous strength; it took 10 of his men to capture one of them. Another Englishman, Captain Sir Thomas Cavendish, followed Drake's path along the Patagonian coast and through the Strait of Magellan in 1587. On the shores of Brazil he saw what he believed to be the footprints "of a gigantic race, as the measure of one of their foot marks was 18 inches (45.7 cm) long,"[9] but despite hearing their howls from the forest, the giants refused to come out into the open.

Anthonie Knivet, an adventurer who sailed with Cavendish, wrote a vibrant book about his voyages around the world. In it he mentions meeting a Patagonian youth who was already more than 9 feet tall. He also recorded that at Port Desire, on the estuary of the Deseado River he saw "Giants fifteene or sixteene spans of height. I affirme, that at Port Desire I saw the footing of them, by the shoare side, that was aboute foure foote of one of our mens in length; and I saw two of them that were buried newly, the one of them was fourteene spannes long."[10]

These giants were measuring between 9 1/2 to 12 feet tall! Dutch Captain Sebald de Veert sailed through the Strait of Magellan in 1599, and reported seeing giants "whom he thought to be ten or eleven feet high"[11] who were so strong that they tore up huge trees by the roots with great ease. That same year in Patagonia, fellow Dutch explorer Admiral Oliver van Noort encountered natives "of a gigantic stature"[12] who continually made war on the shorter people of the region. In 1614, another Dutch explorer Joris van Spilbergen saw at the Strait of Magellan "a human being of very big stature"[13] while the following year it was reported that Jacques Le Maire and Willem Corneliszoon Schouten dug up some stone cairns on the hills at Puerto Deseado and found "the skeletons of men's bodies ten or eleven feet long."[14]

Four years later, Spanish officers Bartolomé and Gonzalo García del Nodal logged in their journals that on Tierra del Fuego, the bottom of Patagonia, there was "a race of men taller, by the head, than the Europeans"[15] and that the early observations of Magellan had been correct. By the 1650s this area of Argentina had inspired mapmakers to rename the Deseado River "River of Giants." Another "River of Giants"[16] was the Purus River in Amazonian Brazil, as documented by the Portuguese explorer Criste de Acuna, who wrote about the Curigueres, a 12-foot-tall tribe of cannibals. The naturalist William Turner also described a race of 12-foot-tall natives on the coast of Brazil living near the Polata River. The giants of this region were incorporated into Spanish cartographer Juan de la Cruz Cano's detailed map of South America in 1775 (the map contains a Valley of the Giants near Puerto Bueno in Southern Chile and a Bay of Giants in Tierra del Fuego), which was inspired by the numerous sightings explorers were making while cruising down the South American coast.

Captain John Byron, grandfather of the famed poet, made three trips to Patagonia over the course of 20 years, eventually meeting people "of a gigantic stature"[17] that eventually found their way into 18th-century literature. Byron wrote that one of his officers was amazed "upon perceiving himself, though six feet two inches high, become at once a pigmy among giants; for these people may indeed more properly be called giants than tall men."[18] Another one of his officers, Charles Clerke, wrote a letter to the Royal Society that described his meeting with the giant Patagonians that took place after a brief examination by Byron, a tall man who still had to stand on his tip toes to do it: "Examined and measured by Mr. Byron. He represents them in general as stout and well-proportioned, and assures us that none of the men were lower than eight feet, and that some even exceeded nine, and that the women were from seven feet and a half to eight feet."[19]

When Captain John Byron returned home in 1766 after circumnavigating the globe in the HMS *Dolphin*, rumors spread that he had seen the 10-foot-tall giants of Patagonia. English artist and novelist Horace Walpole published *An Account of the Giants Lately Discovered: In a Letter to a Friend in the Country*, cashing in on the giant craze that was sweeping England at the time. Charles de brosses, the prolific French historian, writes in his 1756 *Historie des navigations aux terres australes*:

> The coast of Port Desire is inhabited by giants fifteen to sixteen palms high. I have myself measured the footprint of one of them on the riverbank, which was four times longer than one of ours. I have also measured the corpses of two men recently buried by the river, which were fourteen spans long. Three of our men, who were later taken by the Spanish on the coast of Brazil, assured me that one day on the other side of the coast they had to sail out to sea because the giants started throwing great blocks of stone of astonishing size from the beach right at their boat. In Brazil I saw one of these giants which Alonso Díaz had captured at Port Saint Julien: he was just a boy but was already thirteen spans tall. These people go about naked and have long hair; the one I saw in Brazil was healthy-looking and well-proportioned for his height. I can say nothing about his habits, not having spent any time with him, but the Portuguese tell me that he is no better than the other cannibals along the coast of La Plata.[20]

During the closing years of the 18th century, modern science and a new wave of religious dogma sparked a change in society, which was now being told that the Indians of Patagonia were very tall men but not giants. This was due to the giants being forced higher into mountains to avoid being exterminated.

South America is a huge country, full of rugged mountains and never-ending rivers that flow into impregnable misty rainforests. There's also a mass array of megalithic wonders, adobe pyramids, and stone artworks that defy explanation. In the high mountainous regions of Peru, where the legendary Inca once ruled before the conquistadors arrived, there are gigantic stone walls and lost cities that could have only been built by giants. Much like what the Aztecs told the Spanish when they arrived at Teotihuacan, the Incas told conquistador Francisco Pizarro: The giants built this long before they arrived. But Pizarro only had eyes for gold, and unlike most other Indian nations the Spanish had come across, the Incas were awash in the sacred precious metal. This sealed their fates, as Pizarro and the rest of his army eventually wiped them off the face of the earth.

But the legends of ancient Peru remained, as did the physical evidence of the once-mighty giant race that lived there. The late historian Glenn Kimball, PhD, writes about his viewing of a giant Peruvian mummy hidden away in a private gold museum in Cuzco:

> Clearly there were giant kings in Peru. Who knew about these giant kings still remains speculative. . . . I had no dating for the Peruvian Kings themselves. This was a private gold museum and not likely to allow me, or anyone else for that matter, to do any testing that might threaten the ownership of this golden treasure. . . . The actual mummified head of the crowned king in the photograph is almost twice as large as my own and I wear the largest hat of anyone in my acquaintance. When we were invited to the private gold museum to begin with I was expected to be dazzled by gold. However, it dawned on me the minute I walked

> through the door that the size of the head, and indeed his whole body, was the unique feature of this king. The gold was impressive, but the size of the man was something more impressive than gold.[21]

Since the author passed away in 2010, the exact location of this 9 1/2-foot-tall giant mummy resting in a private Peruvian gold museum is anybody's guess. Garcilaso de la Vega, Spanish conquistador and influential poet, chronicled the legends of Peruvian giants after returning from South America a battle-hardened, bitter soul. The Spanish conquest of the Americas was harrowing enough to provide the future poet all the emotional depths needed to be a great scribe. He was also an astute historian; in the *Royal Commentaries of the Incas* he recounts Pedro de Cieza's history of the giants:

> As there is in Peru a story of some giants who landed on the coast at the point of Santa Elena, in the vicinity of the city of Puerto Viejo. . . . The natives, repeating a story received from their forefathers from very remote times, say that there came from across the sea on reed rafts that were as large as big ships some men that were so big that an ordinary man of good size scarcely reached up to their knees: their members were in proportion to the size of their bodies, and it a monstrous thing to see their enormous heads and their hair hanging down about their shoulders. Their eyes were as large as small plates. . . . This is the account they give of the giants,

> and we believe that it happened, for it is said that very large bones have been found and still are found thereabouts and I have heard Spaniards say they have seen pieces of teeth which they thought must have weighed half a pound when whole, and who had also seen a piece of a shin-bone of wonderful size, all of which bears witness to the truth of the incident.[22]

Even a National Geographic-funded expedition in 1997 unearthed a series of tombs rich with the bones of 1,500-year-old "unusually tall young men" surrounded by metal works, ceramics, and llama skeletons. Although they ran the headlines in their February 15th, 2001 issue as "Tomb of 'Giants' unearthed in Peru,"[23] what they really said was that the Moche Indians were suffering from Marfan syndrome and they were really only 6 feet tall. No further discussion has evolved concerning this discovery since, despite the misleading headline, the skeletons weren't actually giant.

If National Geographic wanted to shine a light on the supposed giant past of South America, they would have no shortage of starting points. Consider the astonishing ruins at Tiahuanaco and the machine-carved megalithic stones at neighboring Puma Punku, all of which defy logic and can be attributed to a lost race of giants or ancient aliens. There are clear examples of machined tool markings and cuts on these stones that could have only come from advanced drills of the highest capabilities—tools that we know didn't exist during that time period.

The supposed builders of the monuments were the Aymara Indians, who didn't even have the manpower to move 20-ton stones

A group of monolithic blocks at Puma Punku that were fastened together with special clamps. Notable features at Puma Punku are T-shaped architectural clamps, which are composed of a unique copper-arsenic-nickel bronze alloy. These T-shaped clamps can also be seen at the base of the nearby Akapana pyramid at Tiahuanaco.

hundreds of miles from their quarries. Not to mention Tiahuanaco lies 12,500 feet above sea level, in a region incapable of supporting a population proficient enough to produce such vast works. Nevertheless, despite their architectural difficulties, the megalithic curiosities litter the Bolivian country side for hundreds of miles.

When Francisco Pizarro arrived looking for gold, the Inca told him that Tiahuanaco had been built by a race of giants, called the "Huaris," before the "period of darkness" and was already in ruins before their own civilization began. In his article "The Geoglyphs of Tiahuanaco" researcher David E. Flynn writes:

> At Tiahuanaco, immense stone works were joined with modular fittings and complex breach-locking levels that have never been seen in any other ancient culture. Many of the blocks were joined together with "t" shaped metal clamps that were poured into place by a portable forge. According to engineers, one of the largest single stones ever to be moved and put into building anywhere on earth (about 400 tons) was transported to Tiahuanaco from a quarry over two hundred miles away. This feat is more incredible when one realizes the route of transport was through a mountain range up to 15,000 feet. . . . The historian Arthur Posnansky studied the area for over 50 years and observed that sediment had been deposited over the site to the depth of six feet. Within this overburden, produced by a massive flood of water sometime around the Pleistocene

> age (13,000 years ago) fossilized human skulls were unearthed together with sea shells and remnants of tropical plants. The skulls have nearly three times the cranial capacity of modern man and are displayed in the La Paz museum in Bolivia. An ancient shoreline was etched into the hills surrounding Tiahuanaco that had been lifted out of the horizontal plane. Additionally there were lime deposits on the surface of the exposed megaliths, indicating that they had been submerged in water.[24]

Incan myths attribute the creation of Tiahuanaco to the giants, who in turn had been created by Viracocha, the god who lived in the heavens. But Viracocha grew disappointed at these giants and turned them into stone before flooding the world until every living thing drowned. This mighty flood was called "uñu pachacuti" by the Inca. After the waters had settled, legend says that Viracocha rose from the bottom of Lake Titicaca to preside over the creation of a new species of men. Miraculously, despite the force of uñu pachacuti, the wondrous stone cities and pyramids were still standing as a monument to the giants' existence.

Images from the 1903 expeditions to Tiahuanaco show a megalith block that had been detached or thrown from the Tiahuanaco complex, its surface barring the scars of rushing water. Ocean sediments with characteristics associated with the glacial flooding event that occurred more than 12,000 years ago are deposited all around the massive fragmented out-of-place block. More massive stone

The ancient megalithic Kalasasaya temple at Tiahuanaco.

Machine-drilled holes at Puma Punku.

Machine-carved rock at Puma Punku.

Ruins at Puma Punku 2.

mysteries lie scattered less than a mile away at the mind-boggling ancient site of Puma Punku. Flynn continues:

> Less than a mile from Tiahuanaco, at a place named Puma Punko, immense stone ashlars, some in the 200 ton range were scattered and tossed like a child's building blocks in an episode of unparalleled seismic violence. Posnansky believed that it was more ancient than Tiahuanaco and modern researchers have suggested that both sites may have been built over previous cultures with antiquity stretching back tens of thousands of years. . . . Inca civilization founding myths of giants and world deluge agree with similar legends from the Maya, Olmec and Aztec cultures of Mexico.[25]

The Aymara admitted that the city had lain in ruins for thousands of years before the Incas stumbled across its abandoned stone province. Despite this admission, archaeologists ignore the claims of the indigenous Bolivians and impose their own claims that the Aymara built Tiahuanaco around 400 CE. But the Aymara, like the Incas, both truthfully claimed that Tiahuanaco was built by giants in the age before the floods. This is a scenario some archeologists like Arthur Posnansky theorized based on the dating of the astrological alignments and the fact that Lake Titicaca was once a salt-water sea thanks to the littering of fossilized salt-water seashells on its shoreline. (Try saying that five times in a row.)

The lake is a mysterious host to a range of oceanic types and treasures, as fishermen nets have caught mysterious golden statues

Arthur Posnansky at Tiahuanaco in 1903.

and out-of-place siluroids, cyprinoids, and seahorses. This means this ancient city might have been a one-time ancient seaport whose accompanying land mass was lifted more than 3 miles in the sky thanks to massive earthquakes and the great deluge.

There's also the abundance of giant skeletons and elongated skulls, which have been found at and around the ancient Tiahuanaco area. One of the first stars of feature-length documentaries about exploring lost worlds like the Amazon in the early 1900s was the famous English explorer Captain J. Campbell Besley. With a crew of 11 that included scientists and Hollywood golden-age cinematographer John K. Holbrook, the team set out in 1913 from Lima, Peru, to explore and film the mysterious lost cities of Peru. They eventually traversed uncharted regions from which no known white man had returned from. While searching for the source of the Amazon River, they found the rotting bodies of missing American explorers Mirko Seljan and Patrick O'Higgins. By the time Besley returned to New York more than half of his footage had been either lost or stolen, including the shots of the giant skeletons and lost cities built of massive stones that he said would be impossible to build without modern machinery. Besley's story went national as the *New York Times* reported:

> Capt. J. Campbell Besley, who returned from South America last February with the news that he discovered a lost city of the Incas, arrived in New York recently from his second expedition. Capt. Besley and his party found relics of a giant prehistoric race. One of their finds is an incomplete skeleton, including the skull, of a

> human being who must have been eight feet tall. Other curiosities of great interest were human skulls thought to be four or five thousand years old on which trepanning operations had been performed. These were found in Bolivia, in the Inca ruins. A tradition among the Indians of Peru and Boliva makes the ancient race a race of giants, said Captain Besley.[26]

It seems the earliest scientific and archaeological reports were pretty much convinced that Tiahuanaco was an extremely ancient city that predated the local native inhabitants and was most likely built by a lost race of giants before the great flood. The prominent Dr. Otto Buchtein thought so after studying Tiahuanaco in the 1930s.

> The soil above where they were found in sand and Dr. Buchtein says this indicates that the city of Tiahuanaco was for long time covered with water, and that this was the cause of the wonderful preservation of the articles. Among the discoveries is a large number of skeletons of human beings. The bones were scattered about, and the jawbones were often a yard away from the skulls to which they belonged. While in the museum I saw thirty or forty perfect skulls, which were practically the same as within a few years after the death of their owners, now more than 8,000 years ago. Those skulls are different from any now known. They are of enormous size, and they indicate a race of giants. They slope back from the eyes almost to the crown, reminding one of

> the flathead Indians of North America. The jawbones are heavy, and the teeth, after their rest of eighty centuries, are still almost perfect. It seemed strange to look at the grinning molars and to peer into the eyeless sockets of these men of 8,000 years ago.[27]

Communications engineer and former low-level NASA employee Maurice Chatelain writes about Tiahuanaco in his 1988 book *Our Cosmic Ancestors*, touching on Immanuel Velikovsky's controversial theories about the moon being closer to Earth in the past, which caused humans to be much bigger.

> It seems to be quite sane, because it is in harmony with all the legends and especially with the mysterious stories about giants who lived at the time of the big moon. Even the Bible tells us about them. We now have a mystery to solve. What's the relation between the existence of giants on the Earth in the past that no one, including the Church, has ever doubted, and a closer bigger moon? In my opinion, there is a clear cause-and-effect relationship. A powerful, close and big moon would have reduced the weight of the human body. It so happens that in Tiahuanaco, giant human skulls have been discovered that must have belonged to men nine to ten feet tall. No one denies the existence of giant animals in the past. We have the bones to prove it. Even if at the present we have only a few skulls and tibias of giant men and not too many of their tools, there is little

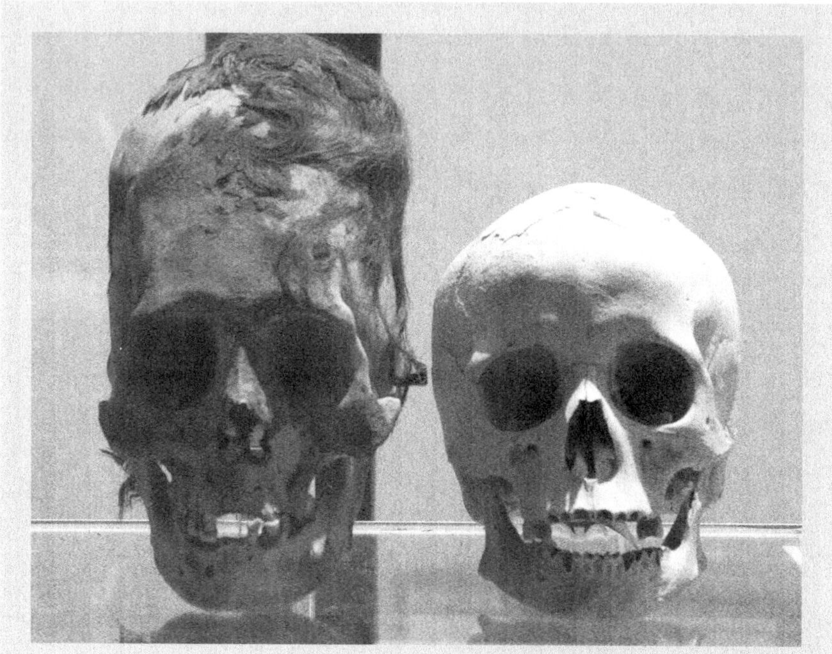

Elongated red-headed skull of Paracas, Peru, next to a normal-sized skull.

> reason to dismiss the theory of closer moons and giants upon the earth. It is only natural that first there were giant animals and then huge men.[28]

The antiquity of the Americas is impressive, as are the strange artifacts the natives of South America left behind. These relics go far beyond the topic of giants and fly straight into headwinds of the ancient alien theory. (Or at least the theory that mankind was a lot more advanced in ancient times then we give them credit for.) Take, for instance, the golden statues of Colombia that are clearly depicting flying jets. How about the other golden artifacts that resemble some sort of ancient earth-moving or tunneling machines? Were these the machines that helped build the ancient megalithic cities of Tiahuanaco and Teotihuacan? Were the ancient giants the inheritors or inventors of this lost technology? And what about the mysterious depictions of six-fingered and six-toed giants that have been discovered throughout the Americas? The ancient Patagonia giants left us a petroglyph of a six-fingered hand in a chilly cave on the southern edge of Argentina. Another petroglyph of a six-fingered hand can be seen north of Patagonia at the Parque Nacional Sete Cidades in Brazil. This national park holds more than a thousand rock paintings dating back 6,000 years, some of which even depict giants with six fingers. The Waorani tribe of Equador has shown to produce tall males with superior genetics, some even having six fingers on each hand and six toes on each foot, unusual birth traits often associated with the ancient giants. It's interesting that this tribe hails from Ecuador, a country where recent archaeological excavations have supposedly revealed a lost city of giants.

CHAPTER 10

Ecuador's Lost City of Giants

As we've now seen, the tradition of a lost race of giants was a universal theme among the Indians of the Americas during the time of the Spanish conquest and was recorded in one form or another by the historians, eyewitnesses, and writers of the time. Conquistador Pedro de Cieza de Leon left Seville at the age of 14 as a stowaway in a Spanish galleon in search of adventures in the New World. He wandered the Andes from 1532 to 1550 where he survived numerous hardships on his way to befriending the indigenous people of Peru and Ecuador. De Leon was able to learn the history of the land, as well as the customs and beliefs of the natives, which he recorded and wrote about in his travelogues. According to his 16th-century writings, de Leon became close with Ecuador's Manta Indians, one of the indigenous tribes of coastal Ecuador, which is where he learned about these mysterious ancient giants. Pedro de Cieza de Leon writes about another tribe of giants who were cannibalistic and practiced the cone-head shaping practice that was popular among a lot of the South American natives:

> All these Indians also eat human flesh. Some of them use bows and arrows, and others staves, clubs, darts, and lances. Towards the north of Cali there is another province, bordering on that of Anzerma, the natives of which are called Chancos. They are so big that they look like small giants, with broad shoulders, robust frames, and great strength. Their faces are large and heads narrow; for in this province, in that of Quinbaya, and in other parts of the Indies, when a baby is born, they force the head into the shape they may choose; thus some grow up without an occiput, others with a raised forehead, and others with a very long head. This is done when the child is just born, by means of certain small boards fastened with ligatures . . . certain Spaniards were sent to guard the road between Anzerma and the city of Cali. These men encountered certain of these Chancos, who had come down to kill a Christian who was going to take some goats to Cali, and one or two of the Indians were killed. The Spaniards were astonished at their great size.[1]

At the end of his inquiry into the phenomenon of the Americas, Pedro de Cieza de Leon surmises that "we may gather, that since so many persons saw and affirmed these things, these giants really did exist."[2] Appropriately, all of the Indian tribes of Ecuador share the same ancient legends about a race of giants that once invaded their coastal South American shores. The Catholic priest Juan de Velasco wrote about these Ecuadorian giants in his book *History of the Kingdom of Quito in South America,* published in 1841 by the printing press of the local government. Velasco's ancient history of Ecuador has yet to be translated and published in English, but thanks to Google translator we can get a fairly accurate translation in a matter of minutes. Velasco's translated text tells how the giants came to the province of Manta and drove out or killed the original inhabitants of the country. Velasco was basically repeating the same story as told by the Mexican historian Pedro Gutiérrez de Santa Clara in the late 1500s, who must have been privy to de Leon's writings considering all three were basically rehashing the same tale.

The Peruvians also share a similar legend of giants coming ashore to wreak havoc and eat the locals before God smote them with fire from the heavens and bright flashes of light. In 1543, the governor of Port Viejo, Juan de Olmos, organized excavations where the natives claimed the giants had been destroyed and "found such large ribs and other bones that, if the skulls had not appeared at the same time, it would not have been credible they were of human persons. . . . Teeth then found were sent to different parts of Peru; they were three fingers broad and four in length . . . from that time forward the native tradition of giants was believed."[3]

In 1570, Spanish priest Jose de Acosta recorded the discovery of giant bones found at Manta and Puerto Viejo that verified the legends of the local Arica Indians, who claimed that wicked giants had come from the sea to make war until they were consumed by fires from heaven. The Carta Indians of northern Ecuador also share the same legends about these giant cannibalistic invaders. Francisco's brother, the conquistador Pedro Pizarro, certainly had images of giants filling his head after entering the ancient megalithic fortress of Sacsayhuaman in Peru. The site was built with massive megalithic blocks that defy explanation and was by designated by Pedro Pizarro as the work of giants. He writes:

> On top of a hill they had a very strong fort surrounded with masonry walls of stones and having two very high round towers. And in the lower part of this wall there were stones so large and thick that it seemed impossible that human hands could have set them in place . . . they were so close together, and so well fitted, that the point of a pin could not have been inserted in one of the joints.[4]

The megalithic masonry in Egypt also has large stones so precisely placed that a human hair can't fit in between them. Are the same giant builders responsible?

Diego the Elder, another conquistador and first European discoverer of Chile, interviewed hundreds of different Indian tribes in an effort to construct the history of the Andes. He retold the exact same story as the other historians: that a race of giants came ashore at the Point of Santa Elena and preceded to dominant the landscape until being destroyed by the fiery wrath of God. It appeared that some of these giant bones were rediscovered in 1928 by railroad workers who were rigging a cave for demolition in Manta. The fact that these giant human remains measuring more than 8 feet tall were

Corner blocks in Khafre's valley temple.

discovered entangled within stalagmites on a petrified floor only adds to the extreme age of the bones. Artifacts and rumored lost cities from this era were discovered off the coasts of Ecuador and Peru in the 1940s by research divers studying ancient marine fossils. The legendary scribe of ancient mysteries Harold T. Wilkins sets the scene.

> When I was at Santa Fe de Bogota, in Colombia, just before the present World War, I met a Senior Mufioz, a haciendero who owns an estate on the seashore not far from Guayaquil, Ecuador. He sent a diver to fish up statuettes from a drowned and very ancient city lying under water just off shore. (The age of this ancient civilization is not known.) The diver came up with artistic statuettes of men and of women whose hair was dressed in very Egyptian fashion! They had the same curiously long slanted eyes as you find in frescoes in the tombs of the Pharaohs. On their breasts were jewels carved in stone . . . Maybe, the drowned race, like their highly civilized contemporaries the Tiahuanacuans, were ancient American colonists from the vast, sunken, highly civilized continent of the mid-Pacific, called Rutas, in the pagoda traditions of old Hindustan, and which, they say, was disrupted by a series of terrific earthquakes and a deluge, sinking it far under the ocean, in a day, "before the Himalayas existed."[5]

Another lost city with visible pillars was discovered off the coast of Peru on October 29, 1965, by the oceanographic ship Anton Bruun. It was led by Dr. Robert J. Menzies of Duke University, who discovered the pillars in the Milne-Edward trench, a depression at the depths of 19,000 feet. Dr. Menzies surmised that the ruins could be those of an ancient lost city and that his discovery could be "one of the most exciting discoveries of this century, insofar as ruins go. Some of the columns are half buried in mud while others stand upright. Many of them appear to have a kind of writing on them."[6] The discovery was initially reported by the highly respected *Science News*, in its April 9, 1966 issue.

> Strange carved rock columns, shown on this week's front cover, some with writing on them, have been sighted by cameras six thousand feet under the sea off the coast of Peru. (Photo credit: Duke University) Dr. Robert J. Menzies, director of ocean research at the Duke University Marine Laboratory, Beaufort, North Carolina utilized a mobile deep-diving vehicle. Two upright columns, about two feet or more in diameter, were sighted extending five feet out of the mud. Two more had fallen down and were partially buried, and another angular squarish block was seen, said Dr. Menzies. . . . The sunken columns are located about fifty five miles off the city of Callao, the port of Lima, capital of Peru. The oceanographer had come across the mysterious sea pillars accidentally, while foraging around for specimens of a small mollusk. His expedition had found sixty thousand specimens of sea animals and taken a thousand underwater photographs before it stumbled across the sunken ruins.[7]

Giant axe-heads in the Museum of Aboriginal Cultures, Cuenca, Ecuador.

Giant axe-heads in the Museum of Aboriginal Cultures, Cuenca, Ecuador.

Giant axe-heads in the Museum of Aboriginal Cultures, Cuenca, Ecuador.

This story, like many others concerning out-of-place artifacts and ancient lost cities was never heard about again.

Honduras also had its fair share of giant discoveries and mysterious lost cities.

> Stories of fossilized remains of huge animals and eight-foot men in Central America, and native legends about their owners have provided another job for a South American scientific expedition. The western Hemisphere has been remiss to contributions in paleoanthropology so when the director of the American museum of natural history heard that Paul L. Vance, New Orleans engineer and amateur explorer, had seen strange skeletons in Spanish Honduras, there was a flutter in scientific circles. Gregory Mason of the university of Pennsylvania museum, head of a South American expedition looking for strange monkeys in quest for a theory of man's beginnings, has been asked to investigate the reports. Vance, who spent twenty three years in the tropics scouting for banana plantations and railroad rights of way told Mason of strange things. At Olauchita, Honduras, he said he found in the sloughed bank of a creek fossilized bones between thirty and thirty-five feet long. The "thing" had a skull about a yard long, huge hind legs and short front ones. Natives said it was the remains of "el Abuelo de los iguanas," the grandfather of the Lizards. Ball and socket type bones six to nine feet long were seen in the bed of the Rio

> Colorado, Vance said. And in a cave on the hacienda of Don Mariana Leiva, ex-president of Spanish Honduras, in Barbara he found on a rock platform eleven normal sized skeletons, and one, he judged to be that of a man about eight feet tall.[8]

Honduras is home to the "lost city of the monkey god," a mythical place that was discovered by explorer Theodore Morde in 1940 only to be forgotten about, dismissed as non-existent, and then miraculously rediscovered as a real city by the press in 2013. Morde was an interesting character, a former spy who supposedly died by hanging himself in the shower as well as allegedly dying in a car crash in London. His tale of finding a lost city in the Central American jungles with giant monkey statues was sensational at the time, but Morde reported seeing vast amounts of gold and silver as well as other strange artifacts with depictions of ancient giants. Unfortunately, flooding prevented Morde from excavating at the time and he died a mysterious spy's death before returning to the lost city. Or did he? Morde and any of his associates would have had 70 years to loot the place, which seems likely considering that the new reports concerning the lost city fail to mention any signs of gold or out-of-place artifacts.

Another lost city has been reported in the highlands of Ecuador, in an area well known for its legends and tales of ancient giants. They're even calling it the lost city of giants! Legends from Ecuador claim that ancient giants abandoned their great stone cities before dying out in the distant past. Naturally, these cities were eventually swallowed up and devoured by the jungles, leaving little visible traces of their existence. Hiding in plain sight, albeit covered with lush green vegetation, one of these lost cities was rediscovered by a team of Ecuadorian adventurers in 2012. Bruce Fenton writes about the initial discovery before joining in on the crusade a year later.

> On the first attempt they became lost, yet fate took a lucky turn, they actually stumbled on a second megalithic site, a strange stone platform situated on the edge of a small river. Scattered about on the jungle floor and in the water itself were a multitude of artefacts and human engineered stone objects. As yet these artefacts have not been matched to any known culture and even their previous functions remain a mystery for the most part. Soon after this the same group launched a second attempt for the megalithic wall in their photograph, this time successfully reaching the site. Thanks to our own efforts to make the public aware of this incredible discovery (or rediscovery even) images and video from the expedition and from others that followed have since sent shock waves through the global archaeological community. No expert has been able to offer an explanation for who might be responsible for this site nor when it could have been constructed. Quite simply it is not reasonable to think these sites were built in the dangerous interior of the Llanganates, rather it only makes sense to assume the structures were built at a time when the jungle was not present and have since been overgrown.[9]

The Wall of the Giants in Ecuador.

This lost stone city is considered sacred to the locals, who speak of incredible tales relating its building to a race of lost giants. Indeed, huge stone tool-like axes and giant skeletons have been found within the vicinity of the complex, which is blanketed by jungle foliage, misty rains, and flowing rivers. Even a large pyramid-shaped edifice measuring 80 meters at the base and 80 meters high, with steep inclined 2-ton megalithic block walls can be seen rising out of the Ecuadorian jungle. Most of the stones are perfectly aligned, with sharp edges that seemingly appear to have been sculpted by giant human hands. Of course the Ecuadorian Ministry of Culture, along with mainstream scholars from the University in Guayaquil investigated the site in 2013 and concluded it was just another natural formation. This blatant attempt at covering up the complex made it impossible to secure funding for further excavations. Yet the precision of the stones, cement-like vitrified materials found within them along with their precise arrangements, and the presence of several circular drilled holes in some of them prove these megalithic wonders weren't the result of natural formations.

In 2014, British anthropologist Russell Dement and his research team claimed to have unearthed six giant skeletons ranging between 7 and 8 feet tall near the site in Ecuador. Dement, who has allegedly studied the history of the area for more than two decades, told Ecuadorian website *Cuenca High Life* that he was inspired to search the area thanks to the local legends of ancient giants. He believes the tall skeletons he discovered were proof of these tales and sent the bones for analysis back to Freie Universitaet in Berlin, Germany, which supposedly funded his research expedition. However, the supposed anthropologist Dement hasn't provided any photographs of the skeleton and his name doesn't appear during a Google Scholar check, which leads most to believe that it's a probable hoax playing off the lore of Ecuadorian giants. This doesn't admonish the fact that giant bones have been discovered in Ecuador along with the ancient traditions of giants, as archived by the majority of the indigenous tribes and the Spanish. Plus, there's also the obvious megalithic ruins pointing to ancient giant involvement in the Ecuadorian amazon. Bruce Fenton, author of a book about giants in Ecuador and a firsthand explorer of the megalithic Ecuadorian ruins wrote a response on blogger Jason Colavito's page about the giant mysteries in question:

> I will tell you this, a few months ago I was living in Bahia de Caracas, coastal Ecuador, a region that is associated with very old reports of fossilized giants. A local man told me a tale about a fairly recent discovery, near to Bahia, made by a foreign team of researchers, led there by locals. They supposedly found two or three sets of skeletons, in a cave hidden in a rock face, that were each around 2.5 meters (8 feet 2 inches) in height. Dating suggested 16th century. The skeletons were apparently seized by Banco Central and shipped abroad.[10]

As we've seen throughout the course of the book the proof of giants as real-life beings that once existed in the Americas is pretty conclusive. Whether being in physical form, as in the shape of bones and skulls, or in the vast mythologies and histories of the natives, we can rest assured that ancient giants were present in the Western Hemisphere both before the great floods and after. We've also seen how the physical proof of these giants has been suppressed purposely by the Smithsonian in order to maintain their church-like grip on the false timeline of history. If we continue to accept that giants never existed then we too will suffer a similar fate, as new generations will fail to dig through the smoky hazes of history, content with believing the same lies as their predecessors while they in turn become the future myths of a human-less robot-dominated utopia. The history of Earth is a shared history for all of us, regardless of race, religion, color, or creed, and we should embrace all of the mysterious events in the past that make up this collective consciousness as we move forward to an even stranger and mysterious future.

NOTES

Introduction

1. "'Red Deer Cave People' Bone Points to Mysterious Species of Pre-Modern Human." *Science Daily*. University of New South Wales. December 17, 2015. *www.sciencedaily.com/releases/2015/12/151217151544.htm*
2. Julian Ryall. "Fishermen Discover Fossil From New Type of Primitive Human." *Telegraph*. January 28, 2015. *www.telegraph.co.uk/news/worldnews/asia/taiwan/11373522/Fishermen-discover-fossil-from-new-type-of-primitive-human.html*
3. Joseph Castro. "Homo Floresiensis: Facts about 'The Hobbit.'" *LiveScience*. January 15, 2016. *www.livescience.com/29100-homo-floresiensis-hobbit-facts.html*
4. Jaime Shreeve. "This Face Changes the Human Story. But How?" *National Geographic*. September 10, 2015. *http://news.nationalgeographic.com/2015/09/150910-human-evolution-change/*
5. Adam Benton. "Homo Rudolfensis: Finally Shown to be a Separate Species?" *Evoanth*. August 12, 2012. *www.evoanth.net/2012/08/09/homo-rudolfensis-finally-shown-to-be-a-separate-species/*
6. Rebecca Morelle. "New Species of Ancient Human Found." *BBce*. May 28, 2015. *www.bbce.com/news/science-environment-32906836*

7. Michael Greshko. "DNA Reveals Mysterious Human Cousin With Huge Teeth." *National Geographic*. November 16, 2015. *http://news.nationalgeographic.com/2015/11/151116-denisovan-human-anthropology-ancient-dna/*
8. Mark Prigg. "Mystery of Our 145 'Alien' Genes: Scientists Discover Some DNA Is NOT From Our Ancestors and Say It Could Change How We Think About Evolution." *Daily Mail*. March 13, 2015. *www.dailymail.co.uk/sciencetech/article-2994187/Mystery-alien-genes-Scientists-discover-DNA-NOT-ancestors-say-change-think-evolution.html*
9. Brien Forester. "DNA Test Results: Paracas Skulls Are Not Human." *Ancient-Code*. December 26, 2015. *www.ancient-code.com/dna-test-results-paracas-skulls-are-not-human/*

Chapter 1

1. Frank Joseph. *Atlantis in Wisconsin: New Revelations About the Sunken Lost City* (Lakeville, Minn.: Galde Press, 1995).
2. "Petroglyph of a Sailing Boat." *Institute for Megalithic Research*. December 8, 2009. *http://megalithicresearch.blogspot.com/2009/12/petroglyph-of-sailing-boat-copper.html*
3. Bryan Hill. "Lovelock Cave: A Tale of Giants or a Giant Tale of Fiction?" *Ancient-Origins*. May 15, 2015. *www.ancient-origins.net/myths-legends-americas/lovelock-cave-tale-giants-or-giant-tale-fiction-003060*
4. "Michigan Copper in the Mediterranean." *www.rocksandrows.com/copper-trade-3.php*
5. John Winthrop. *A Journal of the Transactions and Occurrences in the Settlement of Massachusetts and the Other New-England Colonies, From the Year 1630 to 1644* (Hartford, Conn.: Elisha Babceock, 1790).
6. J.W. Powell. *12th annual report of the bureau of Ethnology to the secretary to the Smithsonian 1890–91* (Washington, D.C.: Government Printing Office, 1894).
7. Ibid.
8. Ibid.
9. J. Taft. *The Dental Register* (Cincinnati, Ohio: Sam'l A. Crocker and Co., 1892).
10. Ibid.

Chapter 2

1. Alvar Nunez. *Spanish Explorers in the Southern United States: Narrative of Cabeza de Vaca* (New York: Barnes & Noble, 1959), 28–29.
2. Walter Malone. *Hernando de Soto*. (New York: G.P. Putnam's Sons, 1914), 401.
3. "Huge skeleton found in Florida." *The Advertiser*. May 18, 1925. *http://greaterancestors.com/huge-skeleton-found-in-florida/*
4. "Fishermen tell of skeletons 8 feet long buried in Florida." The *New York Times*. June 9, 1936. Reproduced in "8 foot giants in Miami." *http://greaterancestors.com/8-foot-giants-in-miami/*
5. "Giants inhabited Florida in the Year 123,084 B.C." *Smyrna Daily News*. January 5, 1917. Reproduced in "Vero Beach giants–12 feet tall." *http://greaterancestors.com/vero-beach-giants-12-feet-tall/*
6. Greg Allen. "Florida fossil hunter gets credit for big find." *NPR*. July 26, 2011. *www.npr.org/2011/07/25/137549198/florida-fossil-hunter-gets-credit-for-big-find*
7. Virginia Steen-McIntyre, et al. "Geologic Evidence for Age of Deposits at Hueyatlaco Archeological Site, Valsequillo, Mexico," *Quaternary Research*, 16 no. 1 (1981).
8. "Giant skeletons are uncovered in Florida." *The Woodville Republican*. Aug 27, 1927. Reproduced in "Giant skeletons are uncovered in Florida." *http://greaterancestors.com/giant-skeletons-florida/*
9. "Workmen discover Ancient Sepulcher." *Ludington Daily News*. December 12, 1924. Reproduced in "7 foot giants in Boynton Florida." *http://greaterancestors.com/7-foot-giants-in-boynton-fl/*
10. Eileen Schulte. "Giants of the Past." *Tampa Bay Times*. July 18, 2008. *www.tampabay.com/features/humaninterest/giants-of-the-past/706261*
11. "Race of Giants once inhabited the Florida Peninsula." *Journal Gazette*. January 20, 1922. Reproduced in "9 foot human skeletons discovered in St. Petersburg, Florida." *http://tnephilim.blogspot.com/2013/05/9-foot-human-skeletons-discovered-in-st.html*
12. David Derbyshire. "The Lost Giants of Georgia." *Science Channel*. September 16, 2014. Reproduced from "The Unexplained Files: Season 2–Episode 8." *www.sciencechannel.com/tv-shows/the-unexplained-files/videos/the-lost-giants-of-georgia/*
13. Richard Gray. "Asteroid impact triggered sudden cooling on Earth 12,800 years ago—and may have killed off the mammoths." *Daily Mail*.

July 31, 2015. *www.dailymail.co.uk/sciencetech/article-3181425/Asteroid-impact-triggered-sudden-cooling-Earth-12-800-years-ago-killed-mammoths.html*

14. Doug Bolton. "DNA discovery unearths 'unknown chapter in human history' in Europe 15,000 years ago." *Independent.* February 5, 2016. *www.independent.co.uk/news/science/population-change-shift-upheaval-europe-discovered-by-scientists-a6855336.html*
15. Robin Whitlock. "Five Huge Bronze Age axes discovered in a field in Jutland, Denmark." *Ancient-Origins.* June 7, 2015. *www.ancient-origins.net/news-history-archaeology/five-huge-bronze-age-axes-discovered-field-jutland-denmark-003190*
16. Paul E. Hoffman. "A New Voyage of North American Discovery: Pedro de Salazar's Visit to the Island of Giants," *The Florida Historical Quarterly* 58, no. 4 (1980): 415–426.
17. Lucian Lamar Knight. *A Standard History of Georgia and Georgians, Volume 1.* (Chicago: The Lewis Publishing Company, 1917), 31.
18. "Monster Skulls and Bones." The *New York Times.* April 5, 1886. Reproduced in "Cartersville 14 foot giants." *http://greaterancestors.com/cartersville-14-foot-giants/*
19. "Find Giants' skeletons." *Oakland Tribune.* January 27, 1904. Reproduced in "Winnsboro, Louisiana 12 foot giants." *http://greaterancestors.com/winnsboro-louisiana-12-foot-giants/*
20. "Race of Giants Found in underground Tomb under 'Old Stone Fort' in Tennessee." *Hartford Weekly Times.* March 30, 1872. Reproduced in "Ancient Cave Dug Under, Old Stone Fort," Tennessee Yields Giant Human Skeletons." *http://moundbuilder.blogspot.com/2013/12/ancient-cave-dug-under-old-stone-fort.html*
21. "3 huge skeletons of humans found." *The Washington Post.* April 24, 1932. Reproduced in "3 huge skeletons of humans found." *http://greaterancestors.com/ripley-tn-3-huge-skeletons/*
22. Kevin E. Smith. "The Williamson county Giant (aka A Pleistocene Mega-Human)," *Middle Cumberland Archaeological Society Newsletter* 38 no. 5 (2013): 2–6.
23. Kevin E. Smith. "The Williamson county Giant (aka A Pleistocene Mega-Human)," *Middle Cumberland Archaeological Society Newsletter* 38 vol. 5 (2013): 2–6.

Chapter 3

1. J. Franklin Jameson. *Spanish explorers in the United States 1528–1543: Expedition of Coronado.* (New York: Charles Scribner's Sons, 1907), 301.
2. George Parker Winship. "The Coronado Expedition 1540–1542," *Bureau of Ethnology* (1896): 485.
3. "Ancient Burying Ground Uncovered." *The New Sentinel.* April 19, 1926. Reproduced in "Skeletons found indicate that race of Giants once lived on Sycamore Creek." *http://tnephilim.blogspot.com/2013/05/giant-human-remains-discovered-alongs.html*
4. "Giant skeleton found up Arizona Ranch." *Weekly Journal Miner, Prescott, Arizona.* August 9, 1911.Rreproduced in "Prescott Arizona Giant Skeleton." *http://greaterancestors.com/prescott-arizona-giant-skeleton/*
5. "8 foot giant skeleton found near Silver City." *El Paso Herald.* April 19, 1915. *www.newspapers.com/newspage/42593591/*
6. "Giant skeletons found." The *New York Times.* February 11, 1902. Reproduced in "Old burial ground yields Giants no less than 12 feet tall in New Mexico." *http://greaterancestors.com/old-burial-ground-yeilds-giants-no-less-than-12-feet-tall-in-nm/*
7. Ibid.
8. "8'6" Utah Giant." *Corbett's Herald.* September 19, 1891. Reproduced in "Giant human skeletons unearthed in Utah." *http://gianthumanskeletons.blogspot.com/p/giant-human-skeletons-unearthed-in-utah.html*
9. Phillip Coppens. "America's Nazca lines." Accessed on June 4, 2016. *http://philipcoppens.com/intaglios.html*
10. Nick Redfern. "The Death Valley Giants." March 26, 2012. *http://mysteriousuniverse.org/2012/03/the-death-valley-giants/*
11. "Biggest Giant Ever Known." *The World.* October 7, 1895. Reproduced in "Biggest Giant Ever Known." *http://tnephilim.blogspot.com/2013/04/giant-human-nephilim-mummified-remains.html*
12. "Important Historical find in California." *The Citizen.* July 28, 1911. Reproduced in "Contra Costa County, more than 7 feet tall." *http://greaterancestors.com/contra-costa-county-more-than-7-feet-tall/*
13. "Best-Preserved Skeleton of Extinct Tribe Hauled from Channel." *Oakland Tribune.* June 10, 1912. Reproduced in "Newspaper Accounts of Giants." *www.jasoncolavito.com/newspaper-accounts-of-giants.html*

14. "Find Bones of a Giant in a California Cave." *L.A. Times*. September 3, 1916. Reproduced in "Giant human skeleton discovered in a California cavern." *http://thenephilimchronicles.blogspot.com/2014/01/giant-human-skelelton-discovered-in.html*
15. "Primitive Man, Ten Feet Tall, Is Unearthed." *The Vancouver Sun*. August 18, 1922. Reproduced in "Articles on Giant Skeletons part 1." *http://nephilim-hunters.com/articles-on-giant-skeletons-part-1/*
16. "Skull of Great Size." *The Sunday Oregonian*. March 13, 1910. Reproduced in "Great Skull and a Gun." *http://greaterancestors.com/great-skull-and-a-gun/*
17. Andy White. "The 'Giant' skeletons from Ellensburg, Washington: A closer look." December 9, 2014. *www.andywhiteanthropology.com/blog/the-giant-skeletons-from-ellensburg-washington-a-closer-look*
18. "The Remarkable Story of a Gold Hunter in the Belt Mountains of Montana–from the *St Paul Pioneer Press*." *The Sun*. July 21, 1889. Reproduced in "Articles on Giant Skeletons part 1." *http://nephilim-hunters.com/articles-on-giant-skeletons-part-1/*

1. Chapter 4⊠James A. Clifton. "How dogs came to the Indians." Accessed on June 4, 2016. *www.samoyed.org/dogind.html*
2. Donald N. Yates. *Old World Roots of the Cherokee*. (North Carolina: McFarland and Company, 2012), 78.
3. Nelson Lee. *Three Years Among the Comanches*. (Albany, N.Y.: B. Taylor, 1859), 149.
4. Ibid.
5. Fanny Bandelier (trans). "Island of Ill-Fate." Houston Institute for Culture. *www.houstonculture.org/devaca/4b.html*
6. "Karankawa tribe." *www.accessgenealogy.com/native/karankawa-tribe.htm*
7. "From Thomas Jefferson to Albert Gallatin." July 12, 1804. *Jefferson Papers*. Accessed June 4, 2016. *http://founders.archives.gov/documents/Jefferson/99-01-02-0058*
8. "Where did Chief Joseph get his Mesopotamian tablet?" March 24, 2011. *http://indiancountrytodaymedianetwork.com/2011/03/24/where-did-chief-joseph-get-his-mesopotamian-tablet-24717*
9. Benjamin Daniali. "A common history of Assyrians and Native Americans." January 9, 2010. *www.assyriatimes.com/assyrian/knowledge/a-common-history-of-assyrians-and-native-americans/3401*

Chapter 5

1. John R. Swanton. *Early history of the Creek Indians.* (Washington: Government Printing Office, 1922), 45.
2. William L. Saunders. *Colonial Records of North Carolina.* (Raleigh, N.C.: P.M. Hale, 1882), 982.
3. Dave Cain. "Giants in our Midst? Tall Skeletons Reported Found in Marion County, WV." *www.bibliotecapleyades.net/gigantes/Marion County.html*
4. Richard Thornton. "Native Americans of the Shenandoah Valley." *Examiner.com,* September 5, 2011. Reproduced in "The Fort Loudon Skeletons." *www.accessgenealogy.com/native/the-fort-loudon-skeletons.htm*
5. "Finding Skeleton of Giant." *The Nebraska Advertiser.* November 19, 1897. Reproduced in "7 feet 6 inch Giant Iowa Skeleton." *http://greaterancestors.com/7-feet-6-inch-giant-iowa-skeleton/*
6. Hugh Newman. "Top ten giant discoveries in North America." January 18, 2016. *www.ancient-origins.net/unexplained-phenomena/top-ten-giant-discoveries-north-america-005196?nopaging=1*
7. Ibid.
8. "Alleged Discover of the Body of a Giant." *Ashburton Guardia* VIII, no 1715 (1887). Reproduced in "Articles on Giant Skeletons part 2." *http://nephilim-hunters.com/articles-on-giant-skeletons-pt-2/*
9. "The Giants of Appalachia." *http://appalachianmagazine.com/2014/09/26/the-giants-of-appalachia/*
10. "Tooth of Prehistoric Human found." *Los Angeles Herald.* January 12, 1917. *http://cdnc.ucr.edu/cgi-bin/cdnc?a=d&d=LAH19170112.2.471*
11. "Giants' Bones in Mounds." *The New York Times.* July 14, 1916. Reproduced in "Scientists Unearth Relics of Indians Who lived 700 Years Ago." *http://greaterancestors.com/7-foot-skeletons-found-in-pennsylvannia/*
12. Eric Hrin. "Eight footer from Troy, Pennsylvania." October 24, 2013. *http://greaterancestors.com/8-footer-from-troy/*
13. "Two Very Tall Skeletons." The *New York Times.* August 10, 1880. Reproduced in "11'3" Inch Skeletons York, Pennsylvania." *http://greaterancestors.com/113-skeletons-york/*
14. Karen Ordahl Kupperman. *Captain John Smith: A Select Edition of His Writings.* (Chapel Hill, N.C.: University of North Carolina Press, 1988), 160.

15. "Indian graves yield Shenandoah Relics." *New York Times*. June 18, 1924. Reproduced in "Berryville, Virginia. Giant Skeletons." *http://greaterancestors.com/berryville-virginia-giant-skeletons/*
16. "Giant's Axe." *West Virginia Historical Magazine Quarterly* vol 2 (1902): 86. Reproduced in "Skeleton 7' 8" and a large axe." *http://greaterancestors.com/skeleton-7-8-and-a-large-axe/*
17. "Skeletons of a stone age man are dug in Connecticut." *The Evening World*. August 19, 1922. Reproduced in "Skeletons of a stone age man are dug in Connecticut." *http://tnephilim.blogspot.com/2013/06/skeletons-of-stone-age-men-are-dug-up.html*
18. "Bones reviewed by Scientists." *The Pittsburgh Press*. December 24, 1922. Reproduced in "Peer revicwed 8 footer." *http://greaterancestors.com/peer-reviewed-8-footer/*
19. "Maryland Skeletons." *The Logan Republican*. October 20, 1906. Reproduced in "Ancient Giant race discovered in Maryland." *http://thenephilimchronicles.blogspot.com/2013/08/ancient-giant-race-discovered-in.html*
20. "Bones of unusual size found in Harlem, New York." The *New York Times*. September 7, 1904. Reproduced in "Bones of unusual size found in Harlem, New York." *http://greaterancestors.com/bones-of-unusual-size-found-in-harlem-new-york/*
21. "Big Skeletons in the Bronx." The *New York Times*. March 15, 1903. Reproduced in "Big boys from the Bronx." *http://greaterancestors.com/big-boys-from-the-bronx/*
22. David Warner Mathesin. "The Smithsonian Cover Up." *The Mathesin Corollary*. April 27, 2014. *http://mathisencorollary.blogspot.com/2014/04/the-smithsonian-cover-up.html*

Chapter 6

1. Tara Maclsaac. "Anomalous Native American DNA: New tests show Middle East origins?" October 26, 2014. *www.theepochtimes.com/n3/1021858-anomalous-dna-found-in-cherokee-native-american-genetic-research/*
2. "Lost City of Giants–Lost Cities Discovered." *West Coast Times*. November 29, 1871. Reproduced in "Lost city of giants discovered in Toronto, Canada." *http://tnephilim.blogspot.com/2013/11/lost-city-of-giants-discovered-in.html*

3. "A Petrified Giant." The *New York Times*. August 17, 1885. Reproduced in "Petrified 12 foot human giant skeleton discovered in British Colombia." *http://gianthumanskeletons.blogspot.com/2014/01/petrified-12-foot-human-giant.html*
4. "Find Skeleton 7 feet tall in Manitoba." *Calgary Daily Herald*. March 16, 1935. Reproduced in "Giant Axe-head from Manitoba." *http://greaterancestors.com/giant-axe-head-from-manitoba/*
5. Jennie Cohen. "Giant ancient camels roamed the Artic." March 5, 2013. *www.history.com/news/giant-ancient-camel-roamed-the-arctic*

Chapter 7

1. "The Aztecs and the ancient giants of Mesoamerica." Accessed July 24, 2016. *www.ancient-code.com/the-aztecs-and-the-giants/*
2. "Teotihuacan and Mica: What is Mica, a powerful radioactive insulator doing in monuments that date back thousands of years?" Accessed July 24, 2016. *www.ancient-code.com/teotihuacan-and-mica-what-is-mica-a-powerful-radioactive-insulator-doing-in-monuments-that-date-back-thousands-of-years/*
3. Fray Diego Duran. *The Aztecs*. (New York: Orion Press, 1964), 5–6.
4. Ibid.
5. Joseph de Acosta, trans Edward Grimston. *History of the Indies, Vol. II*. (New York, Burt Franklin, 1970), 453–454.
6. "Fernando de Alva Ixtlilxochitl." Accessed July 24, 2016. *www.ancientamerica.org/library/media/382chapter11.htm*
7. Adrienne Mayor. *Fossil Legends of the first Americans*. (Princeton, N.J.: Princeton University Press, 2007), 88.
8. Louis Edward Hills. *Historical Data from Ancient Records and Ruins of Mexico and Central America*. (St. Louis, Mis.: Wisconsin Historical Society, 1919), 9.
9. Bernal Diaz, trans J.M. Cohen. *The Conquest of New Spain*. (New York, Penguin Books, 1963), 181.
10. Ibid.
11. "Giant Skeletons in America, Mexico." *http://nephilim-hunters.com/articles-on-giant-skeletons-part-1/*
12. Ibid.

13. "Blond Giant remains found." *Kentucky New Era*. January 5, 1921. Reproduced in "Blond Giant remains found." *http://greaterancestors.com/2-7-mummies-and-an-8-skeleton/*
14. "Smithsonian Amazed at Discovery of 6 1/2-Foot [Up to 8-foot] Mummies in Caves." *Sasquatch Chronicles Blog*. Accessed June 5, 2016. *https://sasquatchchronicles.com/smithsonian-amazed-at-discovery-of-6-12-foot-up-to-8-foot-mummies-in-caves/*
15. Ibid.
16. Ibid.
17. "Cave in Mexico gives up the bones of an ancient race." The *New York Times*. May 4, 1908. Reproduced in "Cave Skeleton 8'11."" *http://greaterancestors.com/cave-skeleton-8-11/*
18. "1 Chronicles 20:6." *http://biblehub.com/parallel/1_chronicles/20-6.htm*

Chapter 8

1. Original source: Works issued by the Hakluyt Society, no. 90. Markham, Clements R., ed., trans. *The letters of Amerigo Vespucci and other documents illustrative of his career.* Translated with notes and an introduction by Clements R. Markham. London: Printed for the Hakluyt Society, 1894. Selected Americana from Sabin's Dictionary of books relating to America, from its discovery to the present time, 6298–6299. Vespucci, Amerigo. *The First Four Voyages of Amerigo Vespucci*. Reprinted in facsimile and translated from the rare original edition (Florence, 1505–6). London: B. Quaritch, 1893.
2. Frederick Dodson. "Underwater ruins and large skulls in the Bahamas." *www.ancient-atlantis.com/underwater-ruins-bahamas/*
3. "Lost City found beneath Cuban waters." December 7, 2001. *http://news.bbce.co.uk/2/hi/americas/1697038.stm*

Chapter 9

1. Antonio Pigafetta. *Magellan's Voyage: A Narrative Account of the First Circumnavigation*. (New Haven, Conn.: R.A. Skelton, 1969), 1:46–47, 50.
2. Francis Drake and Francis Fletcher. *The World Encompassed*. (London, Hakluyt Society, 1854), 56, 40, 41, 47, 49, 51, 68, 93.
3. Ibid.
4. Ibid.

5. Charles Darwin. "Letter to J.S. Henslow, April 11, 1833." Darwin correspondence program. *www.darwinproject.ac.uk/letter/DCP-LETT-204.xml*
6. "Biggest Race of Men in the World." July 30, 1899. *http://cdnc.ucr.edu/cgi-bin/cdnc?a=d&d=SFC18990730.2.87*
7. Tina Hesman Seay. "Human DNA found in Neanderthal woman." February 17, 2016. *www.sciencenews.org/article/human-dna-found-neandertal-woman*
8. Sarmiento de Gamboa. *Viaje al Estrecho de Magallanes por el Capitán Pedro Sarmiento de Gamboa en los años de 1579 y 1580.* (Madrid: Imprenta Real de la Gazeta, 1756), LVI.
9. Robert Kerr. *General History and Collection of Voyages.* (James Ballantyne & Co, 1824), chap. III, Sec. 1.
10. Purchas. *Haklvytvs posthumus Vol IV.* (London: H. Fetherston, 1625), 1232.
11. Robert FitzRoy. *Narrative of the surveying voyages of His Majesty's Ships Adventure and Beagle between the years 1826 and 1836.* (London: Henry Colburn, 1839), 102.
12. Ibid.
13. Joris Van Spilbergen. *The East and West Indian mirror: being an account of Joris van Speilbergen's voyage round the world (1614-1617).* (London: Hakluyt Society, 1906), 39, 41.
14. Jean Le Maire. *Relación diaria del viage de Iacobo Demayre y Guillermo Cornelio Schouten.* (Madrid: Bernardino de Guzman, 1619), 9.
15. *Narrative of the surveying voyages of His Majesty's Ships Adventure and Beagle between the years 1826 and 1836.* (London: Henry Colburn, 1839), 102.
16. Clements Markham. *Expeditions Into the Valley of the Amazons, 1539, 1540, 1639.* (London: Hakluyt Society, 1859), 107.
17. John Hawkesworth. *Account of the Voyages of the Southern Hemisphere.* (London: Cadell, 1773), 12, appendix vii.
18. Ibid.
19. Ibid.
20. Charles Debrosses. *Historie des navigations aux terres australes.* (Paris: Durand, 1756), 343.
21. Glenn Kimball, PhD. "Giants of the royal Incas," *Ancient American* 5 no. 34: 36-38. *www.bibliotecapleyades.net/gigantes/SAm.html*

22. Garcilaso de la Vega. *Sodomite Flesh Eating Giants in Peru by Garcilaso de la Vega-El Inca. Royal Commentaries of the Incas* (In 2 Volumes). University of Texas Press, 1966. Accessed on June 5, 2016. *www.reformation.org/giants-in-peru.html*
23. Jennifer Mapes. "Tomb of 'Giants' unearthed in Peru." February 15, 2001. *http://news.nationalgeographic.com/news/2001/02/0215_moche.html*
24. David E. Flynn. "The Geoglyphs of Tiahuanaco." February 24, 2008. *www.bibliotecapleyades.net/arqueologia/esp_tiahuanaco8.htm*
25. Ibid.
26. "Capt. J. C. Besley Returns with BONES OF EIGHT-FOOT MAN." October 17, 1914. *New York Times. http://query.nytimes.com/gst/abstract.html?res=9E05E4D7143FE033A25754C1A9669D946596D6CF*
27. "Recent excavations on Andean Plateau." August 02, 1914. *http://nebnewspapers.unl.edu/lccn/sn99021999/1914-08-02/ed-1/seq-17/*
28. Maurice Chatelain. *Our Cosmic Ancestors.* (Flagstaff, Ariz,: Light Technology Publishing, 1988).

Chapter 10

1. Clements Markham. *Travels of Pedro de Cieza de Leon.* (London: Hakluyt Society, 1864), 186–194.
2. Ibid.
3. Ibid.
4. Pedro Pizzaro. *Relation of the Discovery and Conquest of the Kingdoms of Peru, Vol. 1-2.* (New York: Cortes Society, 1921), 272.
5. Harold T. Wilkins. "Mysteries of Ancient South America." (London: Rider & Co., 1947), 20-21.
6. Brad Steiger. *Atlantis Rising.* (Lakeville, Minn. Galde Press, 2007), 81.
7. Barbara Tufty. "Found in the Pacific," *Science News* 89 no. 15 (1966): 239.
8. "Explorer Hunts Fossilized Remains of Huge Animals, 8-Foot Men." *Reading Eagle.* August 4, 1933. Reproduced in "Honduras–Giant animals and 8 foot men." *http://greaterancestors.com/honduras-giant-2/*
9. Bruce Fenton. "The Megalithic constructions in the Ecuadorian jungle are not natural features." May 7, 2014. *http://earth4all.net/the-megalithic-constructions-in-the-ecuadorian-jungle-are-not-natural-features/*
10. "Claim: Set of 8 foot tall giant skeletons from 1400-1500 CE found near Cuenca, Ecuador." October 8, 2015. *www.jasoncolavito.com/blog*

/claim-set-of-8-foot-tall-giant-skeletons-from-1400-1500-ce-found-near-cuenca-ecuador

GLOSSARY

Aztec The dominant Mexican culture before the 16th century and Spanish conquest.

conquistador The name used to refer to Spanish conquerors who set out to conquer new territory in the 15th to 17th centuries.

copper oxide ingots A piece of something, in this case metal, that has been reshaped and is ready for processing.

Cro-Magnon An early form of modern human, distinct from more ancient subspecies like Neanderthals and Denisovans.

Denisovan A species also related to modern humans, but distinct from Neanderthals.

dolmen A stone tomb comprised of upright stones supporting a large flat stone.

exhume To dig out something buried.

gigantism Abnormal growth due to hormone imbalance.

henge An ancient circular monument that consists of upright stone or wooden pillars.

Homo sapiens The scientific term that describes modern humans, the only species of humans still in existence.

kangaroo court A court held that does not follow established legal procedures.

Maya A group of indigenous people of Central and South America.

megalith A large stone that is part of an ancient structure or monument.

monolith A large upright stone that is tall and narrow.

Neanderthal A species closely related to modern humans that lived during the Ice Age.

pituitary gland An endocrine gland that controls growth.

plumed serpent An Aztec mythical creature that is part bird, part snake.

pyrotechnic weaponry Materials that undergo a chemical reaction to produce light and heat, such as fireworks.

solstice When the sun hits its annual highest or lowest point in the sky at noon.

tumbaga A metal comprised of gold and copper often used in Central America in pre-Columbian times.

Zapotec An American Indian tribe living near Oaxaca, Mexico.

FOR MORE INFORMATION

Canadian Museum of Nature
240 McLeod Street
Ottawa, ON K2P 2R1
Canada
(800) 263-4433
Website: http://nature.ca/en/home
The Canadian Museum of Nature's collections contain natural history and life science artifacts.

National Center for Science Education
1904 Franklin Street Suite 600
Oakland, CA 94612
(510) 601-7203
Website: https://ncse.com
The National Center for Science Education works with educators, parents, and concerned citizens to defend accurate science education all over the United States from ideological threats.

National Museum of Natural History
10th Street & Constitution Avenue NW
Washington, DC 20560
(202) 633-1000
Website: https://naturalhistory.si.edu

The National Museum of Natural History has exhibitions and research collections on natural science specimens and cultural artifacts.

Royal British Columbia Museum
675 Belleville Street
Victoria, BC V8W 9W2
(888) 477-7977
Website: http://www.royalbcmuseum.bc.ca
The Royal BC Museum has galleries and archives that showcase the natural history of British Columbia, including its cultures.

World Explorers Club
One Adventure Place
Kempton, IL 60946
(815) 253-9000
Website: https://wexclub.com
The World Explorers Club publishes a print magazine and online blog on historical mysteries and ancient civilizations. The club also organizes group trips to sites around the world.

Websites

Because of the changing nature of internet links, Rosen Publishing has developed an online list of websites related to the subject of this book. This site is updated regularly. Please use this link to access this list:

http://www.rosenlinks.com/DAA/giants

FOR FURTHER READING

Bergen, Lars. *Ancient Aliens and the Age of Giants: Through the Wormhole.* Gityasome Books, 2013.

Childress, David Hatcher, and Brien Foerster. *The Enigma of Cranial Deformation: Elongated Skulls of the Ancients.* Kempton, IL: Adventures Unlimited Press, 2012.

Chouinard, Patrick. *Lost Race of the Giants: The Mystery of Their Culture, Influence, and Decline Throughout the World.* Rochester, VT: Bear & Company, 2013.

Coppens, Philip. *The Ancient Alien Question: A New Inquiry Into the Existence, Evidence, and Influence of Ancient Visitors.* Wayne, NJ: New Page Books, 2011.

Dewhurst, Richard J. *The Ancient Giants Who Ruled America.* Rochester, VT: Bear & Company, 2013.

Jones, Lindsay, and Richard D. Shiels. *The Newark Earthworks: Enduring Monuments, Contested Meanings.* Charlottesville, VA: University of Virginia Press, 2016.

Lynott, Mark. *Hopewell Ceremonial Landscapes of Ohio: More Than Mounds and Geometric Earthworks.* Oxford, UK: Oxbow Books, 2015.

Martinez, Susan B. *The Mysterious Origins of Hybrid Man: Crossbreeding and the Unexpected Family Tree of Humanity.* Rochester, VT: Bear & Company, 2012.

Newman, Hugh, and Jim Vieira. *Giants on Record: America's Hidden History, Secrets in the Mounds and the Smithsonian Files.* New York, NY: Avalon Rising Publications, 2015.

Pozzi, Alberto. *Megalithism: Sacred and Pagan Architecture in History.* Boca Raton, FL: Universal Publishers, 2013.

IMAGE INDEX

Introduction

I-1: Red Deer Cave People skull anterior and lateral.
D. Curnoe, J. Xueping, and J. Herries, CC 2.5, via Wikimedia Commons. *https://commons.wikimedia.org/wiki/File:Red_Deer_Cave_people_skull_anterior_and_lateral.png.*

I-2: Homo Floresiensis skull displayed at the Natural History Museum of Senckenberg, Switzerland.
Daderot, CC0 1.0, via Wikimedia Commons. *https://upload.wikimedia.org/wikipedia/commons/d/d1/Homo_floresiensis_skull_-_Naturmuseum_Senckenberg_-_DSC02091.JPG*

I-3: The cave on Flores Island where specimens were discovered.
Lian Bua, CC BY-SA 2.0, via Wikimedia Commons. *https://en.wikipedia.org/wiki/Homo_floresiensis#/media/File:Homo_floresiensis_cave.jpg*

I-4: Homo rudolfensis skull reconstruction displayed at the Museum of Man in San Diego. Durova, CC 4.0, via Wikimedia Commons. *https://commons.wikimedia.org/wiki/File:Homo_rudolfensis.jpg*

I-5: The oldest fossil of the genus *Homo.* Fossil mandible HCRP-UR 501=Homo rudolfensis, original specimen, 2.4 mya, excavated by the German paleo-anthropologist Friedemann Schrenk in Uraha, Malawi.

Gerbil, CC BY-SA 3.0, via Wikimedia Commons. *https://en.wikipedia.org/wiki/Homo_rudolfensis#/media/File:HPCR-UR_501-03.jpg*

I-6: Australopithecus family.
Matheusvieeira, public domain, via Wikimedia Commons. *https://commons.wikimedia.org/wiki/File:Australopithecus_family.jpg*

I-7: The spread and evolution of the Denisovans.
John D. Croft, CC 3.0, via Wikimedia Commons. *https://commons.wikimedia.org/wiki/File:Spread_and_evolution_of_Denisovans.jpg*

I-8: The elongated skulls of Paracas, Peru.
Brien Foerster, CC 3.0, via Ancient-Code.com.
www.ancient code.com/elongated-skulls-traces-of-an-unknown-species/

Chapter 1

1-9: Robert Wadlow's shoe, size 25, compared to a normal men's size 12.
Doug Coldwell, CC BY-SA 3.0, via Wikimedia Commons. *https://en.wikipedia.org/wiki/Robert_Wadlow#/media/File:Wadlow_shoe_compared.jpg*

1-10: An Indian mound at Chillicothe, Ohio.
Rdikeman, CC 3.0, via Wikimedia Commons. *https://commons.wikimedia.org/wiki/File:Hopewell_culture_nhp_mounds_chillicothe_ohio_2006.jpg*

1-11: America's Stonehenge in Salem, New Hampshire.
J. Miers, CC 3.0, via Wikimedia Commons. *https://commons.wikimedia.org/wiki/File:America's_Stonehenge.jpg*

1-12: Entrance to Lovelock Cave near Lovelock, Nevada.
Ken Lund, CC 2.0, via Wikimedia Commons. *https://commons.wikimedia.org/wiki/File:Entrance_to_Lovelock_Cave,_Near_Lovelock,_Nevada_%28529142604%29.jpg*

Chapter 2

2-13: The expedition of Cabeza de Vaca.
Lencer, CC BY-SA 3.0, via Wikimedia Commons. *https://commons.wikimedia.org/wiki/File:Expedition_Cabeza_de_Vaca_Karte.png*

2-14: Illustration of mammoth or mastodon tusks with marks presumably made by humans. Found by E.H. Sellard at Vero man site in 1916.
E.H. Sellard, Wiki Commons.

2-15: Mound B at the Etowah Indian Mounds archeological site in Georgia.
Kare Thor Olsen, CC BY-SA 3.0, via Wikimedia Commons. *https://en.wikipedia.org/wiki/Etowah_Indian_Mounds#/media/File:USA-Georgia-Etowah_Indian_Mounds-Mound_B.jpg*

Chapter 3

3-16: Map of California shown as an island circa 1650.
Johannes Vingboons, public domain, via Wikimedia Commons. *https://en.wikipedia.org/wiki/Wikipedia:Featured_picture_candidates/Island_of_California#/media/File:California_island_Vinckeboons5.jpg*

3-17: A giant on rock art at Canyon Ranch, Winslow, Arizona.
Alan Levine, CC 2.0, via Wikimedia Commons. *https://commons.wikimedia.org/wiki/File:Giants,_Petroglyphs_at_Rock_Art_Ranch.jpg*

3-18: Ten foot tall skeletons of California. *The Washington Times*, July 13, 1908. *Greaterancestors.com.*

Chapter 4

4-19: The Gentle Giant from the Lost Giant and other American Indian tales retold, 1918.
Violet Moore Higgins, public domain, via Wikimedia Commons. *https://commons.wikimedia.org/wiki/Category:The_lost_giant_and_other_American_Indian_tales_retold_%281918%29#/media/File:The_lost_giant_and_other_American_Indian_tales_retold;_%281918%29_%2814778563882%29.jpg*

4-20: The Gentle Giant.
Violet Moore Higgins, public domain, via Wikimedia Commons. *https://commons.wikimedia.org/wiki/Category:The_lost_giant_and_other_American_Indian_tales_retold_%281918%29#/media/File:The_lost_giant_and_other_American_Indian_tales_retold;_%281918%29_%2814592187830%29.jpg*

Chapter 5

5-21: A 35,000-year-old Cro-Magnon skull located at the Musée de l'Homme, Paris.
120, CC 2.0, via Wikimedia Commons.
https://en.wikipedia.org/wiki/Cro-Magnon#/media/File:Cro-Magnon.jpg

Chapter 7

7-22: Teotihuacan seen from the Pyramid of the Moon.
Peter Anderson, CC 2.0, via Wikimedia Commons. *https://commons.wikimedia.org/wiki/File:Teotihuac%C3%A1n.jpg*

7-23: Teotihuacan's Pyramid of the Sun.
Ricardo David Sánchez, CC 3.0, via Wikimedia Commons. *https://commons.wikimedia.org/wiki/File:Teotihuac%C3%A1n-5946r.JPG*

7-24: The Storming of the Teocalli by Cortez and his troops.
Emanuel Leutze, public domain via Wikimedia Commons. *https://commons.wikimedia.org/wiki/File:Leutze,_Emanuel_%E2%80%94_Storming_of_the_Teocalli_by_Cortez_and_His_Troops_%E2%80%94_1848.jpg*

7-25: Matthew Stirling and his wife Marion with a colossal Olmec head.
Unknown, Wiki Commons.

7-26: Ancient Giant as depicted by the Aztecs.
www.ancient-code.com/the-aztecs-and-the-giants/

Chapter 8

8-27: Pictograph in Pomier Cave 1.
Espeleogrupo, public domain, via Wikimedia Commons. *https://en.wikipedia.org/wiki/Pomier_Caves#/media/File:El_Pomier_-_Cueva_numero_uno.JPG*

Chapter 9

9-28: English sailor offering bread to a Patagonian woman giant.
John Byron, A Voyage Round the World in His Majesty's Ship the *Dolphin*, London, 1767. *http://libweb5.princeton.edu/visual_materials/maps/websites/pacific/magellan-strait/patgonian-giants.html*

9-29: A group of monolithic blocks at Puma Punku that were fastened together with special clamps. Notable features at Puma Punku are T-shaped architectural clamps, which are composed of a unique copper-arsenic-nickel bronze alloy. These T-shaped clamps can also be seen at the base of the nearby Akapana pyramid at Tiahuanaco.
Janikorpi, CC 3.0, via Wikimedia Commons. *https://commons.wikimedia.org/wiki/File:Puma_Punku_foundation_plate_joint.JPG*

9-30: The ancient megalithic Kalasasaya temple at Tiahuanaco.
Marc Davis, Wiki Commons

9-31: Arthur Posnansky at Tiahuanaco in 1903.
Tihuanacu, the Cradle of American Man, Vols. I–II, Wiki Commons.

9-32: Elongated red-headed skull of Paracas, Peru, next to a normal-sized skull.
Brien Foerester, Hiddenincatours.com

9-33: Machine-drilled holes at Puma Punku.
Brattarb, CC 3.0, via Wikimedia Commons. *https://en.wikipedia.org/wiki/Pumapunku#/media/File:Puma_Punku7.jpg*

9-34: Machine-carved rock at Puma Punku.
Brattarb, Wiki Commons.

9-35: Ruins at Puma Punku 2.
Brattarb, Wiki Commons.

Chapter 10

10-36: Corner blocks in Khafre's valley temple.
Horemweb, CC 4.0, via Wikimedia Commons. *https://commons.wikimedia.org/wiki/File:Khafre_valley_corner.jpg*

10-37, 10-38, 10-39: Giant axe-heads in the Museum of Aboriginal Cultures, Cuenca, Ecuador.
All images by Bruce Fenton

10-40: The Wall of the Giants in Ecuador.
Image by Bruce Fenton

INDEX